A WREATH OF GUNSMOKE

by

Sam Gort

Dales Large Print Books
Long Preston, North Yorkshire,
BD23 4ND, England.

British Library Cataloguing in Publication Data.

Gort, Sam
    A wreath of gunsmoke.

    A catalogue record of this book is
    available from the British Library

    ISBN   1-84262-095-9 pbk

First published in Great Britain 1995
by Robert Hale Limited

Published in Large Print 2001 by arrangement with
Robert Hale Limited

Dales Large Print is an imprint of Library Magna Books Ltd.

Printed and bound in Great Britain by
T.J. (International) Ltd., Cornwall, PL28 8RW

ONE

It was high summer and a glorious afternoon. The western distance, bright blue and white-crowned by the streaming peaks of the Laramie range, hung across the heavens like a painting embedded in fine crystal, while the air, filtered by the soft wind blowing off Wyoming's lakes and forests, tasted of life at its fullest. The scene was as near perfect as anything which this world had to offer, and just right, in Sam Creed's opinion, for the meeting that he planned to bring about with Madge Stacey in the next hour. His decision was made. He would be leaving the Union Pacific's department of railroad detectives shortly and was now ready to ask Madge if she would marry him – which she had long ago said she would if he gave up his dangerous job with the railroad company.

Yes, he could see it clearly now. The dear girl had been right all along. It was a poor life for a woman who saw her husband no more than once in several weeks and lived the majority of her days in the fear that he would not come home at all – unless it be in a long wooden box that was accompanied by a mealy-mouthed letter of condolences from U.P's chairman. No, he had to admit that he had been a selfish devil to go on working for the Union Pacific this long. When all was said and done, it wasn't as if the proof of Madge's contentions hadn't been there often enough. He had been wounded twice in the last ten years, had come through a number of ambushes by the skin of his teeth, and had suffered a slightly deformed left hand during one of the several bar-room dust-ups in which he had taken part. It would be best to put the job behind him once and for all. His luck would probably run out if he didn't, and he would go into another of those unmarked graves in the Cheyenne cemetery. At the age of thirty-two, he had no desire to lie dead and forgotten just yet.

Glancing over his right shoulder, Creed raised an eyebrow. His horse – which he was leading across the Cheyenne freight yard – had begun dragging against his hand. The old brute was no doubt feeling lazy. It always did after a ride on the train. And he and the big gelding had just finished a long one from Des Moines to the U.P depot in Cheyenne. It was his plan to walk his mount right out of the yard, and hope that it would give the animal the chance to rediscover why the Almighty had given it four legs. 'Come on, pudding-head!' he urged fondly. 'Get the lead out, will you? Life would be one long rest if you had your way!'

The horse gave him a disapproving snort, and he knew that he was once more hearing the creature's opinion of men who gave up good jobs at the sniff of a petticoat. Horses had their lives better organised than that, and more savvy to go with it. Creed allowed himself a rather grim and knowing little smile. He knew what the gelding had yet to learn. It was going to receive some real bad news before long. They were going into the cattle business, and it would find itself at work every day of the week from dawn till dusk. When a fellow went into business in a small way – with a view to building it up by his own efforts – he had to expect to do the work of two men, and the same rule applied to his horse.

'Well, look who's here!' greeted a rather familiar voice from the left. 'Hello, Creed! I see you're still talking to that black jughead of yours!'

Creed turned his head. He looked towards an open window of the depot's office, which he was at present passing, and saw a thick-shouldered, paunchy, florid man peering out. 'Hello, Mr Binns,' he responded, a touch of acid in his voice as he considered the other's muddy eyes and expensively pomaded head of black hair. For George Binns, the manager of the Cheyenne railroad depot was not one of his favourite people; and this had become particularly true since the disappearance two years ago of a carload of goods salvaged from a train wreck this side of South Pass had given him cause to doubt the man's honesty. In fact Binns had later been selling curtain materials, brooms, and items of hardware out in the Territory which had looked very like those which had vanished, but proving the case had been too difficult and Creed had never brought it to the Company's notice. 'If my horse hears you call him a jughead again, mister, you're liable to go home minus the seat of your trousers. He's sensitive; but you wouldn't know about that, would you?' Creed smiled bleakly, halting his mount for the sake of politeness and hanging a trifle on the bit. 'How are you keeping these days? Wealthy?'

For an instant a malicious glint touched the manager's gaze. 'I work for the same company you do, Creed. We don't often see you in Cheyenne these days. I expect you know there's been a buzz on the wires.'

'Isn't there always?' Creed wondered. 'What about?'

'You.'

'Me?' Creed laughed disdainfully. 'It's a pity those telegraphers of yours haven't got something better to waste their pencils and paper on.'

'The rumour is, you're leaving U.P.'

'For once a rumour is correct.'

'When's it to be?'

'The end of the month.'

'That's still three weeks away.'

'I have that much furlough due.'

'You detectives do all right.'

'You managers do even better,' Creed returned bluntly, taking a certain pleasure in the other's affronted scowl, for the fact that Binns was his superior in the Union Pacific's chain of command no longer seemed to matter a damn to him. 'There's nothing like sitting around in a comfortable office to give a fellow that soft and happy look.'

'I have my privileges,' Binns huffed, 'but I

also have my responsibilities.'

'You and me both.'

'Seems that playing railroad detective has got on top of you, Creed,' Binns jeered. 'Has your nerve gone?'

'Try me,' Creed suggested. 'I won't run away.'

'You're still an employee of this company,' Binns warned. 'It's still in my power to have you fired for gross insubordination. You may have more to lose than you think.'

'Then show me a little respect too,' Creed advised. 'Oh, what the hell! Yesterday is dead, and life's for the living.'

'Sounds to me like you're going to loaf your days away.'

'I wouldn't bet on it,' Creed responded, figuring that he would probably achieve more by avoiding direct confrontation and making a weapon of the simple truth of what he planned for the future. 'It's all right, Mr Binns. You can know what I intend to do presently. I'm going into the cattle business. By the spring of next year, I hope to be shipping stock to Chicago from your depot.'

'So you're going to become a rancher,' Binns observed. 'That's ambitious. It takes capital too.'

'I've got some.'

'I'm not surprised to hear it,' the manager drawled. 'You've always had the name for being a close one with your money.'

'Perhaps. But what I have is all mine, and honestly come by.'

'You'll need a partner.'

'I intend to take a wife.'

Binns frowned momentarily, then a smile that was both quick and taunting appeared on his face. 'This,' he said, 'gets better and better. Who's the unlucky girl, Sam?'

'You probably know.'

'That's what I was thinking,' Binns said slowly, a gloating note in his voice. 'Madge Stacey?'

'How I feel about her has never been a secret in Cheyenne,' Creed said. 'I'm just off to her home, and I'm going to ask her to marry me. Though why I should be telling you all this, I'm damned if I know!'

'Oh, you poor fellow!' Binns exclaimed, his eyes showing a cruel mirth while his voice tried to express a heartfelt pain that was wholly fraudulent. 'Haven't you heard about Madge?'

'Heard what?'

'This is sad!'

'Is she dead?'

'Far from it.'

'Binns!'

'You really don't know, Sam?' the manager pleaded. 'Boy, I thought you'd have been the first!'

'If you were a younger man—'

'You'd drag me out of this window and break my nose,' Binns sighed. 'So you really don't know. That makes me the bearer of sad tidings.'

'Just what the heck are you yammering about?' Creed shrilled, his frustration almost throttling him. 'This is sheer wickedness, Binns, and well you know it! Come to the god-damned point! Tell me!'

'Peace, Sam!' Binns soothed. 'Peace! It's nothing to get het up about. You love her, don't you? You want nothing but her happiness?'

'Yes, that's about the size of it.'

'Fine. Because Madge got married last Saturday. It was quite a turn out.'

For a moment Creed could hardly believe his ears. Then for another instant he thought the manager was joking. But in the second after that he realised that the manager's triumphant leer reflected neither more nor less than the cruel truth. He raised a hand involuntarily, and pressed it to the front of his shirt, feeling as if he had just received a tremendous blow over the heart. 'The devil you say!' he muttered hoarsely. 'Who did she marry then?'

'Hubert Eichmann.'

Creed breathed slowly and deeply. He now felt a nasty suspicion that all this talk, initiated by George Binns – who had no liking for him, and had certainly been under no obligation to speak – had in fact been carefully steered towards the revelation concerning Madge Stacey from the start. For the manager would have realised, on seeing him out in the freight yard – newly arrived from head office in Des Moines, where work was the only subject discussed – that it was almost certain he had heard nothing about the girl's wedding. After all, his potential heartbreak from what appeared to have been this sudden union must have been predictable to anybody who had been aware of the longstanding romantic connection between Madge and himself, and he would hardly have journeyed to Cheyenne with a smile on his face if he had known what had happened. Plainly his manner throughout the foregoing dialogue had confirmed his ignorance and encouraged Binns to produce the most damaging moment he could in which to deliver his bombshell, and likewise the rumour on the telegraph wires might also have been another indicator for the manager. George Binns was sharp – the manner in which he had contrived to stay out of trouble all his life was proof of that – but to play on a man's feelings as he had just done was despicable. He deserved to rot in hell! But vengeful folk of his kind were like that, and this latest piece of nastiness was only to have been expected after the too pertinent questions which Creed had asked about those salvaged goods. Binns had been as guilty as sin all right, and that could only have made his hatred ten times stronger.

'Too bad,' Binns commiserated, his tones still that fraction too sweet. 'But as I said, with things how they were between you and Madge Stacey, I'd expected you to know all about it.'

'Well, I didn't,' Creed said flatly. 'Madge is no letter-writer, and I'm no better in that line.' He lifted his head, for he had assimilated the blow by now and his mind was clearing. He was determined not to let his disappointment demean him further, for there were aspects of this affair that went far beyond his personal feelings. 'What a silly girl Madge is! To marry Hubert Eichmann of all men! A damned jailbird! I didn't even know they'd let the varmint out of Cañon City penitentiary. He was sent there for seven years, and parole had already been denied. When did he get out, Binns?'

'Are you sure it was seven years, Sam?'

'Dead sure,' Creed replied. 'I should know, shouldn't I? It was my investigation of his doings over in Colorado that put him in jail.'

'You'd know all right,' Binns acknowledged. 'If what I heard was correct, Eichmann got out a fortnight ago. It was on parole. Remember, he was a first offender. That would have made a difference, wouldn't it? I believe a first offender can apply for parole after serving half his sentence.'

'True,' Creed said, sleeving sweat off his forehead and gazing heavenwards as if in search of the ultimate answer. 'I suppose Madge felt sorry for him. She's got a big heart, and Eichmann used to be the fellow she turned to when I was out of favour. He's a handsome villain, and she used to insist there was good in him. I know better. Hubert Eichmann is rotten to the core. Madge will live to regret what she's done. You see if she doesn't, Mr Binns!'

15

'It's a done job, Sam,' the manager reminded.

'Do you have to rub it in?'

'You can't run away from the truth,' Binns pointed out sententiously. 'Madge and Hubert are honeymooning down the trail in Ganville. With Eichmann's parents, as the word goes. Why don't you jump on the next train west and visit them? It might do you the world of good to give them your blessing. A belated wedding present wouldn't go amiss. Nor would a garland of flowers for the happy couple.'

'I hope I'm not a vindictive man,' Creed said with feeling, 'but Hubert Eichmann will get neither present nor garland from me. Though some day I may send him a wreath of gunsmoke!'

'Sam, that is poor!' the manager chided. 'Those words sounded mighty like revengeful ones to me. I can assure you the men at head office would be furious if they learned that you had said such a thing publicly. Don't you always like to present yourself as a man a cut above the rest of us?'

'Stow that, Binns!' Creed snapped. 'You're not the public, mister, and what saint ever became a railroad detective anyhow? Put your thinking cap on! How long do you

16

figure Eichmann has it in him to go straight? First offender? That's what the records may say! He was the late Norman Trevelyan's lieutenant, and as evil as his boss. That's the truth of it. Hubert was in to everything. He'll be back robbing the Union Pacific – and any other organisation he can – within a month. I'd stake my life on it!' He slammed his left fist down on the windowsill, causing his horse to start a little. 'Christianny, Binns! Madge Stacey will be a five minute wonder with him! He's been starved of women for a long time, and that's what it's all about with him. Once he's had his fill of wedded bliss, he'll saddle up and ride the round, bringing Norm Trevelyan's boys together again. I've heard the gang are pretty well living together across the line in Colorado anyway. It makes me sick to think about it! What did I put in all that work busting the Trevelyan bunch up for?'

'It isn't your worry any longer,' Binns returned. 'You will be nursing cows soon. Take my tip, Sam, and forget here and now that you were ever a railroad detective.'

'I reckon you do have the right of it there,' Creed admitted a touch grudgingly, the V above his eyes gathering as he gave the mouth of his increasingly restive horse a disciplinary chuck. 'Patience, blast you! We'll be going along soon.'

'You've stood there long enough,' the manager agreed.

'So I have,' Creed said shortly. 'Well, I've done my best by everybody. I can't do any more.'

'That's another thing you shouldn't say in public,' Binns cautioned. 'Sam, you sounded sorry for yourself just then. Folk can't abide a fellow who believes he's been hard done by. Yes, you did fair to middling. It was your Winchester that put paid to Norman Trevelyan and a number of other truly wicked guys. If the Trevelyan gang should ride again, with Eichmann at its head, I don't think it will pose the threat it did before. But let's see how it turns out, Sam. It may yet prove that Hubert's new missus has the trick of putting salt on his tail.'

Creed nodded. 'That's my hope for us all. Well, I'm off, Mr Binns. So long.'

'See you around, Sam,' the manager smirked. 'Go and get drunk. There are plenty more girls in town. They're all the same – I promise you.'

Creed raked the other with a disbelieving eye, then walked away from the office window, heading for the broad gateway at the top of the yard that gave access to the main street. His horse dragged a trifle, playing him up again, and he swore at it across his shoulder. Heck but he felt sapped – and almost ready to believe that he was still asleep on the train and having a bad dream! Then he shook his head at the notion, frowning darkly; for he knew that he was wide awake, and had never been more so in his life before; but those bright colours of half an hour ago had turned dull, and there was no longer any life or sweetness in the Wyoming air. It had all gone stale on him, and he felt that hope belonged to others and had abandoned him for ever. He had aged thirty years in thirty minutes. If he'd only known that all this awaited him, he'd never have come within a hundred miles of Cheyenne this week.

TWO

Clear of the railroad depot, Creed swung into his saddle and gazed down the main street towards the middle of the town. People were about in numbers, and there was plenty doing, yet he found little to attract him in it all. And there was the worst of it. He had been brought up in Cheyenne – and his parents lay buried in the town cemetery – but he no longer had the feeling that he belonged to the place, or even wanted to belong to it. It had been Madge from start to finish. She had been the essence of this town for him. Even his ranching plans had had the girl at their heart and, now that her spirit had been removed from that central point, what was left foundered on the fact of Cheyenne. The vision was dead; everything had been washed out; and he felt as aimless as any one of the ten thousand saddletramps who regularly criss-crossed the West in search of a perhaps unrecognised salvation they could never find.

Creed's horse stirred beneath him. It didn't like his mood. More, its idleness had passed and it wanted to be doing. But he didn't. That was the last thing right now. He had dollars enough in his money-belt to buy himself a first-class ticket to hell on Satan's flyer. If he wished he could drink himself stupid, gorge himself sick, or exhaust himself in a brothel full of whores. Yet he hadn't sufficient spark left in him just now to give a serious thought to any of it. All he needed, when last came to last, was a corner in which to lick his wounds. He would go and find one.

He turned his horse off the beaten way. There was a gap between two of the houses on his left. Prodding his mount, he sent it galloping into the space and across the rough, grass-tufted ground beyond. Ahead of him now were the woods, and he prayed that the trees would soon absorb him. As a kid, he had always found peace in the tall timber and, with it, revival of his spirit and energies. If the forest didn't do the trick, he might sit down on this deadfall or that and blow his brains out. Damn, Madge Stacey! How could she have done this to him? And all without a word of warning!

Drinking more and more deeply of his

bitterness, he galloped across the mile or so of intervening land and entered the forest. He found himself accusing now, and making out a case against Madge to suit his own mind. He even began to hate and wish harm where he had once loved so deeply. This horrified him, for he was basically the fairest of men and always sought a balanced judgment. Even when he was one of life's victims. It was this saving grace that sobered him and, as he asked himself how much of his suffering was truly down to Madge, his incipient hatred evaporated, for the answer was none at all. The fact was that he had always been a slave to his work, and had tended to play fast and loose with the girl because of it. He had expected her, because he saw himself and his job as of more importance than she, to put up with whatever he had handed out. The arrogance of it! How could he have been so blind to his own uncaring use of Madge's affections? She had merely served as an emotional interest in the background of his life. He felt shamed. He had used Madge Stacey in almost every meaning of the word. Altogether, coming back here to find her married was what he had deserved. So he had better be a man and swallow the dose. There — it was over and done with.

Guiding his horse to a spot where a fallen cedar lay, Creed drew rein and dismounted. Sitting down on the deadfall, he began to consider the bleak tomorrow that he had made for himself. It no longer seemed to matter what he did with his life. A man's real worth was in what he did best. Well, he had always been among the Union Pacific's best track detectives and ought not to give it up. If he returned to Des Moines on the next eastbound train, head office would probably let him withdraw his notice to quit. It might hurt his pride a bit, but that wouldn't do him any harm. 'Never go back' had always been good advice, but he had never really left–

The sound of a rifle clapped violently in the silence of the woods, and the bullet seemed to arrive with the force of a sledge-hammer. Creed clutched at his belly and rolled off the deadfall, landing on his side with his knees drawing up. Eyes bulging with shock, he lay there, mouth spewing bile as he waited for his last agonies to begin. Today he would have to be braver than he had ever imagined. It took real courage to die alone with a bullet in your guts.

But then Creed realised that he had not

received a mortal wound. There was pain, yes, but it grew smaller rather than worse. Neither did Creed find his life force ebbing, and it slowly came to him that the bullet had struck the gold pieces packed into his money-belt and failed to penetrate to the flesh behind it. He was at most deeply bruised, and the life was still whole in him.

Getting a new grip on himself, Creed gazed into the undergrowth before him and picked up movement behind a clump of mottled oakbrush. Light glinted on steel as the barrel of a rifle was lowered and blurred features pushed into the space that it had previously occupied. It was obvious that the bushwhacker was unsure as to whether his fallen victim were dead or not, and that he was shoving himself forward to obtain a better view.

Operating at the extremity of his will, Creed tipped upwards onto his knees, drawing his revolver as his torso came erect. He fired instantly at the spot where the face was still dimly in sight. Bits of foliage went flying, but he knew that he had missed his mark, and a scampering of feet a second later told him that his would-be killer was vacating the scene at top speed. Creed tried again, judging the path of his bullet on the sounds still drawing to him, but the rapid trampling of boots and snapping of small branches went on as before – with the slight difference that the noises were now receding and their direction tending to confuse as their echoes bounced off the trunks of the great conifers standing round and about.

Creed thrust himself fully erect. His rage seemed the more intense for his earlier despondency. He hurled himself into pursuit of the bushwhacker, though his injury still hurt him a lot and he realised that he might be wiser to let the rifleman go in the present surroundings. For the forest cover favoured his attacker entirely. But a form of challenge had been issued, and it was not in his nature to back off because the setting was against him and he was at a total loss to know why he should have been fired on. His policy had always been to shoot first and ask questions afterwards. That way a man lived longer and learned more.

Into the oakbrush Creed plunged – bursting through the undergrowth beyond it in the same cavalier fashion – and he emerged in a circle of low-hanging foliage. Ducking now, he bored onwards, and the ground underfoot began to hollow. Checking but slightly as he started to descend, he peered this way and that after any sign that the rifleman had gone into hiding nearby and was ready to shoot it out. But he saw nothing, and let his blind pursuit gain speed again, going for the further wall of the hollow without so much as a zig or a zag to protect himself.

The floor of the forest slanted upwards. Creed climbed for a few moments, then charged through the willow brake at the edge of the depression above. Now he came out in a relatively open place and, towards the further side of it, he saw a shadow diving beyond a stand of hickory wands and realised that, for all the haphazard nature of his pursuit, he had stayed very much on his would-be killer's heels and actually been gaining on the man.

Creed pointed his revolver, inclined to let fly again – though he knew that slugs triggered by a running man seldom brought their target down – but just then, as his soles slammed dully against the moss and leaf mould that formed the surface of the ground beneath them, he picked up a foul smell from not far ahead of him and saw a number of pallid sago lilies huddling amidst their leathery green foliage about a large ring of earth that appeared blacker than the forest shadows.

The word 'bog' loomed in Creed's consciousness. He veered to his left, convinced that he was missing the circle of danger, but he suddenly found himself knee-deep in the morass and realised that his feet had been travelling faster than his wits. He floundered from one leg to the other, trying to free himself as he continued sinking perceptibly, and the sickening odour of methane gas came belching up around him as the top of the swampy place bubbled and popped in the woodland silence.

Putting his gun away, Creed stood motionless, aware that he was already seriously mired and that his wild efforts to help himself were self-defeating, for he was obviously sinking that much faster as he made them. Looking around him, he saw a clump of pussywillows growing out of what appeared to be more solid ground a short distance to his left and, bending over and reaching out, he managed to clutch the growth with both hands and hold on, the illusion of security coming with his effort; but, as he put pressure on the willow and tried to drag himself out of the bog, the roots of the tree tugged away from the loose black soil in which they were embedded and left him floundering anew. So once more the power of his effort to help himself worked in the opposite manner and he slipped several inches deeper into the mire. Up to the middle of his thighs, indeed, and he perceived that he was now hopelessly trapped and felt the horror of a different kind of despair from that which he had experienced before.

Panic seized him, and for several moments he struggled mindlessly, beating at the swamp with his arms and making cowardly noises that shocked him out of his folly. His efforts stilled again, and he watched what was happening to him with eyes that bulged in horror. He was immersed up to his hips, and then up to his waist – and he knew that he was settling faster all the time, and that a few more minutes would see the end of him. Once more terror knotted into his guts, and the hair stiffened on his scalp and nape. 'Help,' he bawled, not caring in the least if his echoing plea brought the bushwhacker back to his spot. 'Help! In God's name – somebody, help me!'

He went on shouting in similar vein, and the reverberations of his voice seemed to flee to the limits of the forest and rise into its roof. Presently animals could be heard fleeing from the fear he was generating, and birds flushed through the highest branches into flight. Creed's prayer for assistance seemed to fill the whole world, yet it went unanswered – even by the unknown enemy – as the still rational part of sinking man's brain feared it must, and he slowly accepted that rescue was beyond the bounds of possibility and he was doomed. But he meant to go on bellowing his lungs out – since the constant release of energy helped – and he promised himself that his last cries would have to be choked into silence by the bog.

Then, like some spirit voice that mocked – yet was plainly human and no less strained and anxious than his own – he heard the tones of somebody nearby demanding: 'Where the devil are you? What's up?'

Creed became instantly silent, listening with all the power of his ears – trying his hardest to work out the position of the speaker.

'Where are you?'

'Down here!' Creed responded. 'Up to my chest in the bog!'

'Keep yelling!' he was advised; and did just that.

There was movement at the edge of the clearing on Creed's right. He saw a small man, dirty in person and disreputably garbed, appear among the bushes there. The newcomer was the type of individual that few would normally have wished to see; but right then no angel from heaven would have been more welcome in Creed's sight. 'You can see how it is with me!' he gasped. 'Get me out of it, for God's sake!'

'Easier said than done, boy!' the other commented, his foxy features immobile as he rubbed a thumb under his sharp little nose. 'Ain't sure what I can do about it!'

'You've got more sense about you than that!' Creed protested.

'It's all very well to talk!' the foxy-faced man returned aggrievedly. 'What help will it be to you if we both get drowned?'

'Get over here!' Creed ordered. 'You have a gunbelt on you! Unfasten the thing and swing it out to me! I'm going to die if you don't!'

The newcomer approached, but held back at a safe distance, a hand at the buckle of his gunbelt. 'How did you manage to end up in that muck? I can't pull you out! You're too big and heavy!'

There was truth in that and, close to death though he might be, Creed could not deny it. 'Have you got a horse?'

'Back there?'
'Far?'
'Too far.'
'It mustn't be!'
'You got one?'
'He is too far!'
'Plumb awful!'

'Just go!' Creed said as quietly and forcefully as he could. 'Get back here as swiftly as you can.'

Foxy-face left at top speed, and the slowly settling Creed tipped back his head and watched him – praying as never before, and almost without being conscious of it – for there was so much half understood and barely determined, with mind clashing on mind and a score of details revolving amidst the doubt as the deciders of make or break. It was a nightmare in the light of day.

The seconds ticked inexorably away. They became a minute. And the minute became two. Tension worked through Creed as a form of heat coupled with pins-and-needles. Still he settled – slowly, slowly. Now the bog held him at the level of his armpits, and his arms lay extended before him on the surface of mire. If this went on much longer–Where was that little man? It seemed to the quivering and shivering Creed that Foxy-face had had time to go to Cheyenne and back by now!

Then Creed heard something over to his right. He tilted his head in that direction. The noises he picked up were definitely those of a horse charging towards him through yonder undergrowth. It might be that the railroad detective was going to survive after all. Provided the mount could be put into position soon enough – and a link provided between it and the sinking man – all could even now be well. But hurry it up. Hurry it!

But Foxy-face proved less of the slouch than it had seemed at first he might be. He arrived beside the morass from the denser woodland in moments only and, though circumspect to the last degree, placed his horse in the best possible position within half a minute more, casting the noose of a lariat out to Creed and winding the loose end of the rope about his pommel. After that it was an easy task for the towing animal to draw three-parts sunken man to safety, delivering him to firm ground much like an expertly extracted tooth.

'You awright, son?' Foxy-face asked, coming to stand over the rescued railroad detective.

'I'm fine,' Creed assured him, shaking off the lariat and scrambling erect – as if to prove himself in a hurry that he still could – and then he stood and wrinkled his nostrils, making noises of disgust at the stink of his own person. 'I need a bath.'

'You sure do,' the other agreed inconsequentially. 'Close call.'

'If I never have another like it,' Creed said frankly, 'it'll still be one too many. There was me thinking it was my unlucky day. Never know, do you?'

'I'd say not.'

Creed looked down on Foxy-face from the considerable advantage of his six-feet two-inches of height, and a slow, hard smile of recognition started dawning in his eyes as he saw his rescuer clearly for the first time. 'I know you, don't I?'

'Yeah, Creed – just like I know you.' A thin smile settled on the rescuer's stubbly, feral visage. 'Crazy, ain't I?'

'For pulling me out of that pot?' Creed queried, grinning despite himself. 'Depends on your point of view, I guess. Wilfred Mansell, isn't it?'

'That's my moniker.'

'Well, Mansell,' Creed said evenly, 'a train robber and every other breed of criminal bastard you may have been, but you saved my life – and within the law, I'll be eternally grateful. It would have been a hell of a way to go, choking my last in that filth!'

'I wouldn't wish it – even on a railroad detective,' Mansell responded, without raising a word of objection to any word that Creed had spoken previously; for he had been a member of the Trevelyan gang that the U.P man had broken up a few years ago and was still wanted in many parts of the West. 'I heard a gun go off, Creed. Did you fire it?'

'It was fired at me,' Creed answered, rubbing the spot behind his money-belt where the hurt left by the bullet's blow was now playing him up again. 'The bullet hit me too, but luckily some metal turned it. I ran after the bushwhacker – got careless, I guess – and ended in the mire. Thank God you were around to hear my shouts! That was a chance in thousands, I'd say.'

'Again dependin' on how you look at it,' Mansell commented, the pull of his jib expressing an extreme wryness. 'That bullet was intended for me, Creed. It was Les Cable who fired it. He's been hunting me for weeks. I reckon he figured it for pay day when he mistook you for me. Now that was a chance in thousands, wouldn't you say?' He smiled, revealing a mouthful of spiky, rotten teeth. 'At that, Les'd have soon killed you as me.'

'So maybe it was no accident?' Creed queried. 'You guys have no call to like me, and that's a fact. The whole bunch of you, in the Trevelyan mob, would have gone to jail for life if I'd had my way. But I imagine that shot fired at me was just the luck of the moment. Things like that do happen in the circumstances. They're not new.'

'Yeah,' Mansell said, 'I'd bank it happened as it happened. Just a coincidence.'

Creed wiped the slime off his pants with the edges of his hands and dashed the marshy rottenness of it to the ground at his feet. 'What,' he inquired, without raising his eyes from his task, 'would Les Cable be hunting you for, Mansell. You and he used to be pals. You were both top members of Norm Trevelyan's bunch.'

'How right, mister,' Mansell acknowledged. 'When friends fall out, eh? But that's much water down the creek.'

'I see. Or maybe I don't?'

'You don't.'

'Can you tell me?'

'Can I?' Mansell chuckled to himself.

'That's real polite, Creed. Maybe I should save your life more often! Can I, indeed?' He chewed a blue and bloodless lower lip. 'Yeah, I can tell you. I aimed to take it to the county sheriff in Cheyenne anyway. In fact I reckon what I know belongs more with you than Morgan Target.'

'So?'

'Young Hubert Eichmann has brought the survivors of the old gang together again. He did it from jail mostly. Sent out riders where he had to.'

'I'd heard something about it.'

'Then you know Hubert's been paroled?'

Creed shrugged. As a matter of policy, he wasn't prepared to come out with all that he had learned from George Binns, the Union Pacific depot manager, back in town. 'I also heard he's got married.'

'Didn't waste his time when he got out, did he?' Mansell leered. 'The Stacey girl. Your intended, wasn't she?'

'They're both took in and done for now,' Creed said shortly. 'I'm hoping the joys of marriage will keep that hellion out of mischief.'

Mansell chuckled derisively down the front of his collar, then blew a raspberry.

'Not getting all that far, are we, Wilf?'

'Oh, I dunno, Creed,' Mansell said.

'What do you know, Wilf?' Creed inquired sweetly. 'Or are you just stringing me along?'

'We both know very well the gal's just a toy to Eichmann,' Mansell answered. 'He's seen too many fancy drawers to get into a lather over one more pair. He's up to his old games again, and won't be woman-struck for long. There's somethin' big in the wind.'

'And you know what?' Creed suggested.

'Why else would Les Cable want to shoot me?'

'Keep talking, Wilf,' Creed advised. 'Yet there's a big "why" behind this. It'd make more sense if–'

'Those kids don't want me any more,' Mansell cut in bitterly, his tongue audibly breaking free from the restraints that he had so far imposed upon it. 'They say I'm too old and slow for train robbin' and such devilry now. Hube Eichmann sent out from prison to say I was to take my ass off. And me still years from sixty! That riled me up and, like the fool I am, I told Les Cable I'd carry word of Hube's big job to the law. The next thing I knowed, Eichmann had set Cable on me and I had to ride out of Ganville fast. I've been leadin' Les a merry dance since then but, even so, he durn nearly caught up with me a couple of hours ago.' He rubbed his jaw hard. 'Tell you, Creed, I saw the need to get smart again in a real hurry! So I ducked away into this part of the forest. Les is no hunter once you get him into the trees. To my figurin', he's got less bump o' direction than a blind man. I knew I could lose him good and proper again in the heart of the forest, then ride south for Colorado. There's an agein' lady down in Durango who kinda owes me a favour or two.' Once more he rasped nervously at his chin. 'But I ain't sure that's still an option – if it ever was.'

'Oh?'

'Les knowed the lady as well. Also how my mind works.'

'That's no good,' Creed admitted. 'Any notion where Cable is now?'

'Thought I heard him ridin' off north-wards.'

'Only thought,' Creed mused. 'You know the worst of it, don't you. Cable must have heard me shouting for help. If he didn't actually see what had happened to me, he may well have worked out what it was. If he drifts back this way with his gun, for a look-see, we're both in trouble. Wilf, that sidewinder could be watching us right now!'

Shivering, Mansell drew his head down between his shoulders and cast frightened glances all around him. 'You do have a possibility there, boy, and I'm about to make myself scarce.'

'You haven't told me what Eichmann's got cooking yet!' Creed complained, though he was animated as much by curiosity as a sense of duty; since he was off U.P's list of operational detectives and his responsibility here could not be described as more than nominal. Therefore, though he did care who robbed whom, it was only as just another public-minded citizen, and not as a man likely to do anything personally active about it. As he saw it at this moment, the fore-shadowed crimes of Hubert Eichmann and company were indeed the business of Morgan Target, the county sheriff, and he had no right to do more than make himself the repository of whatever information he could gather concerning them. 'Spit it out, Wilf!'

'No,' Mansell said decisively. 'I ain't wastin' any more time here. If Les Cable don't show up further – and my luck holds generally – I'll meet you in the Indian's Head saloon this evening. I reckon you owe me a drink, Creed! It's a risk maybe, but I could sure do with a whisky.'

'You can have a cask of it,' Creed promised. 'But you really ought to tell–'

Turning away, Mansell walked to his horse. He swung into his saddle with plenty of skill and energy. Then, lifting his left hand in quick salute, he spurred off. Fetching round to his right, he entered the trees to the south of the swampy place, all sight of him disappearing within moments.

Breathing deeply, Creed slowly shook his head. This evening wasn't very far away, and he hoped that he would see the little man again – but he didn't feel too confident of it.

THREE

Retracing his steps to the horse that he had recently not expected to see again, Creed gave the animal a friendly pat on the neck and then led it away from the thin forest grass amidst which it had been foraging. Mounting up, he did a little more backtracking through the part of the woodlands by which he had earlier come in and soon rode out of the trees and into the open land beyond. He was in a filthy mess, and stank to high heaven. To think of entering Cheyenne in such a state was not really in the question. He must clean himself up – and fast – in just about any circumstances that would serve.

He knew of a fishing pond a little to the south of town. It wasn't far out of his way, and he rode there, springing down among the bushes at the northern end of the water. Kicking off his boots and removing his gunbelt – where his fouled pistol remained holstered – he dived into the shadowy depths of the pool and swam and wallowed around there for the next ten minutes, only clambering out to strip off his well-soaked clothing and find a piece of soap in a saddlebag to do his laundry.

After thoroughly washing his shirt, trousers and underwear, Creed squeezed the garments half dry and then spread them out on top of a nearby thicket to dry in the sun. Then he jumped into the pool again and had another swim, emerging this time to dry himself on a towel that came from the same source as the soap and dress himself anew in the change of clothing that he always had by him on the trail. Next he cleaned his boots, gunbelt, and weapon – taking plenty of time to do a thorough job – and finally he collected his more or less dry things off the thicket and packed them away. Now, with the sun westering – and his thoughts never far from Wilf Mansell – he climbed on to his horse once more and rode in the direction of Cheyenne, entering the town as an averagely clean specimen of the human race and showing no sign of the frightful ordeal through which he had passed not so many hours ago.

Figuring he still had time in hand before he need go to the Indian's Head saloon and his meeting with Mansell, Creed rode up to the hitching rail outside the barber's shop and there again drew rein. Dismounting, he tied his horse at the rail and then went into the tonsorial, where he asked for a shave, trim, and pomade. The barber wasn't too busy at this time of day, and he used the best of his skills on his customer, going to work liberally with the brilliantine. Satisfied – and feeling that he really made quite a handsome guy – Creed left the barber's shop in the honey glow of the hour and returned to his horse. The brute withdrew a little and put back its ears, treating him like a stranger as he untied it. 'I know,' he said, scowling. 'You preferred me the way I smelled before. There's no pleasing some horses.'

Returning to his saddle, Creed stirred his horse into the slowest of movements up the street. Feeling lack lustre now, he yawned, for the residue of his earlier disappointment still hung about him. He recalled walking here with Madge Stacey, indulging her insatiable love of window-shopping, treating her to soda pop and cookies in Lannigan's restaurant, and generally cutting a caper to keep her amused. There would be no more of that, and it hurt. But at least the worst of his dark mood had gone away, and he could face tomorrow – and whatever it might bring – with reasonable equanimity.

Creed saw the Indian's Head on his left and a short distance before him. The saloon was among the largest in town and had recently been repainted scarlet and gold, while its sign was brand new and had probably been brought in from the East. He was aware that the beers were shipped in from Des Moines, that the girls were hand-picked by the management in New York, and the gambling was more or less honest. A pretty face and a glass of beer would be welcome, and he reckoned that Wilf Mansell and he could spend a pleasant enough spell together in the Indian's Head – even if the wretched little fellow were a limb of Satan and no company for any honest man to seek. It wasn't so hard to tolerate a train robber when he had saved your life. And that was a fact.

Just, then, looking up a trifle, Creed saw Mansell riding towards him. The diminutive crook appeared to spot Creed at the same moment and, putting on a vaguely ingratiating grin, lifted a hand in salute. Creed nodded that touch warily in reply, and was preparing to turn in at the saloon's hitching rail, when a hidden rifle went off. Mansell jerked erect in his stirrups, as if badly startled by the noise, then toppled out of his saddle and came to rest on the street's rutted surface, rising a small cloud of yellow dust in the process.

Stiffening in his own seat, Creed watched as a couple of bystanders made for the shot man on running legs. Then, drawing his Colt, the railroad detective sprang to the ground and turned full circle, eyes seeking the spot from which the bushwhacker had fired into the street. There was a sudden grating noise – which Creed identified as a tile slipping and, his gaze rising abruptly, he saw a tiny deformity appear and vanish down the further side of a rooftop chimney. He tried there and then to identify what part of a figure he had seen up there, but nothing more came into sight – though a further rattling of displaced tiles suggested that the rifleman had just confirmed the effectiveness of his shot from the chimney's cover and was now scrambling down into the lots behind the properties that bordered the northern edge of the main street.

Creed dodged away from his horse. Then he darted into the first alley to which he came on his right. Feet hammering in the narrow place, he soon arrived at the end of the passage and turned to the opposite hand. Slowing, he peered through a muddle of unplanned fences, roughly built sheds and outhouses, linen lines on drying grounds, piles of rubbish, and the clumps of dying elder and rusty oakbrush left by teams of builders who had been forced to work much faster than they should while throwing up the centre of Cheyenne to meet the ever-increasing trade and housing requirements of an expanding population.

Movement was difficult to spot amidst so much detail. Creed checked still further, increasingly baffled by the crude complexity of it all, and he was on the verge of halting altogether and losing his sense of purpose, when a figure leapt from the ground about thirty yards beyond him – hidden at the start by one fence – and heaved himself over the top of another, dropping out of sight down its further side.

Studying the scene to his right for an instant, Creed received the impression that the rifleman had been doing things the hard way. There was a broad band of open ground beyond the limit of the properties. It appeared to run parallel with the full length of the main street. If such were the case, it must provide an easy way of covering the distance which the bushwhacker was traversing with so much effort. True, the killer had started far closer to the back walls of the buildings than had been the case with the railroad detective – and probably felt impelled to flee wherever he saw a sure path ahead – but even so he could have made matters a lot easier for himself had he plunged straight for the open ground adjoining the lots at the very beginning.

Diving out to his right, Creed soon made another left turn, and now, as he had been almost certain would prove the case, the land at the back of town stretched wide open before him. He sped down the sixty yards that he must cover in about a fifth of the time it would have been taken over the lots themselves. Then he saw a space between two buildings on his left and, behind the gap, he glimpsed a man swinging onto horseback. Filling leather, the other saw him and, just short of pushing his rifle into its saddleholster, raised it like a Colt revolver and triggered at Creed, missing him by just a few inches. Then he did indeed thrust the Winchester into leather, and an instant later he was gone – hidden by the building that stood to the right of the railroad detective's present placement.

Again Creed changed position. He raced

through the gap behind which he had seen the bushwhacker. Once beyond the walls that obstructed on either hand, Creed skidded to a halt and peered after the fugitive, for the man was still fully in sight and galloping westwards. His face came round, dark and snarling, and he jerked his revolver and fired behind him as he saw his pursuer gazing after him. Creed heard nothing of the bullet and pulled his own gun, muttering the name: 'Les Cable.' Since he had known the other for years by sight and had no cause to regard him with much but fear and dislike. So, aiming a little high, he triggered a couple of shots after the fleeing rider – expecting to miss at the present range – but, to his surprise, Cable lifted up and lurched forward in his saddle, dropping down again to lie over his pommel in the manner of one who had just received a substantial wound.

Creed fired a third time, attempting to make a job of it, but on this occasion he clearly missed and had to accept that the range was now far too long for any hope of accurate shooting. He thrust his gun away – hoping that Cable had received a mortal injury and would fall off his horse and die before getting far up the trail – then faced about and ran back over the same route that he had used to get here, re-entering the main street through the mouth of the alley by which he had left it.

A circle of blood on the beaten way marked the spot where Wilfred Mansell had fallen, but the badman's body no longer lay upon the ground. Creed felt momentarily baffled as to what had occurred in his absence, but there were men standing around and talking with various degrees of animation among themselves, so he asked what had become of Mansell and was told that the man had been removed to Doctor Nathaniel Sinclair's surgery.

Creed spoke a word of thanks, knowing that Doctor Sinclair's house was the large, red-roofed one on the right-hand side and perhaps fifty yards up the street, and he walked quickly to the building and went in through the iron gate that served a small forecourt. Another five paces brought him to the doctor's front door, and he beat upon it with the side of his right fist, perhaps using more violence than he realised in his suppressed excitement, for he suddenly heard a female voice in the hall beyond call out irritably: 'All right – I'm coming, I'm coming!'

Dropping his fist to his side, Creed stepped back a little and watched the door open before him, a tall young woman with bright blue eyes and soft red hair appearing in the entrance. She gazed at Creed, her gaze lighting with a recognition that also contained faint amusement and a strong dash of irony. 'Sam Creed,' the doctor's daughter said. 'I might have known you'd be involved in this. Somebody said that you had been seen getting off the train from Des Moines this afternoon. Your reappearance in Cheyenne always spells trouble.'

Scowling despite himself, Creed made a dismissive gesture with his left hand. 'They brought Wilf Mansell in here just now, Lois,' he said.

'The shot man?' she responded. 'Yes.'

'Then he's still alive?'

'I believe so – though I wouldn't give much for his chances.'

'It's something anyhow,' Creed said. 'From the way he fell, I feared him dead.'

'You shot him?'

'No, Lois!' Creed protested, frowning again – for there had always been a slight attraction between him and Lois Sinclair, and the doctor's daughter had been gifted with the power to make him feel small and

52

uncomfortable. 'Wilf Mansell was gunned down by a bushwhacker, name of Les Cable, right out there in the street.'

'I see,' Lois said. 'The men were babbling so much when they brought the poor fellow in, I could hardly understand a word.'

'May I come in?'

'You may not.'

'I have a duty here!' Creed said hotly, aware that, strictly speaking, he was lying in the most brazen manner. 'If Mansell is like to die, there's something I must try to get out of him first.'

'You're a violent man, Sam!' Lois Sinclair chided. 'Everything about you carries an air of haste and gunsmoke. If only you had been as good with your school books as you are with a pistol!'

'You misjudge me!' Creed declared in great exasperation, knowing that both his words and his attitude were the worst possible in the circumstances. 'I was done with it all. There – you know. I came back here today to ask Madge Stacey to marry me.'

'What a facer for you!' the red-haired girl observed, not noticeably sympathetic.

'It was my fault,' he confessed. 'I know I'm the only person to blame. You can't just leave a girl suspended and expect her to be there when you're ready for her.' He tut-tutted, fingers working. 'Now – will you let me in, please?'

Lois Sinclair smiled wryly at his 'please'. 'You may be learning, Sam,' she said. 'Are you sure you have a duty here?'

'I feel it so,' he said, his voice carrying a note of honest conviction now.

Nodding, the girl turned away. 'Follow me, Sam.'

Creed pursued her along the hall, praying that Mansell was still alive and that he would find the little fellow conscious.

Lois Sinclair stopped outside a door on the right. A hand upon the knob, she turned and faced him, twisting the door open and stepping aside as she gestured for the railroad detective to enter the room beyond.

'Thanks,' Creed said, passing into a place that was obviously the doctor's surgery, for Wilf Mansell was lying upon the examination couch and the white-aproned Doctor Sinclair was bending over him and studying wounded flesh from which he had cut away a big piece of the outlaw's filthy shirt with a pair of scissors that were still jutting from his cocked right hand. Looking round sharply, the very tall and elegantly formed

54

medico frowned at the newcomer, since the group of townsmen who had presumably carried the wounded man into the house were still present and the surgery was overfilled.

Creed inclined his jaw curtly. Then, disregarding how the doctor clearly felt, walked right up to the couch and bent over the man lying upon it, noting at once that Mansell's eyes were open and that he was breathing in quick, shallow gasps which were filled with the sound of bubbling blood. Mansell was dying for a certainty, and he looked as if he might go at any moment now. 'Hello, Wilf,' Creed said pleasantly. 'We'll have to wait for that drink, eh? Better if you'd tried Colorado. Cable wasn't deceived.'

'Reckon not,' the outlaw gurgled, smiling faintly.

'What was that you were going to tell me, Wilf?' Creed asked, putting just enough pressure into his tones. 'What's cooking in the Eichmann camp?'

Mansell didn't answer, though it was plain from the expression in his fading eyes that he understood well enough, and Creed received the impression that a kind of residual loyalty to his own kind had reasserted itself in the outlaw. For several moments it appeared that the badman would die without voicing any further word that might help the forces of law and order; so, deciding that it could no longer hurt the dying man if he behaved in a brutal fashion, he snarled: 'Hube figured you for a useless old coot, didn't he? He kicked you out into the cold like he would have done any mangy cur that wasn't worth its keep! Are you going to let that polecat get away with it?'

A tiny flash of anger showed in the expiring outlaw's pupils, and his bloodless lips quivered like blue rinds.

'Spit it out, Wilf!' Creed rasped, his presence a commanding and relentless one. 'Next stop hellfire, you know!'

'The eastbound Flyer,' Mansell whispered soul and body straining at the words. 'Wednesday night – July eighth. Big gold shipment – from Sacramento. Cutman's Pass.' There was something else, and the listener doubted it could be much, but the dying man made his last and greatest effort over it. 'Look out for – for Stanley Barstow.' Then his jaw rolled a trifle, his gaze fixed, and it was all over.

The doctor pulled Creed away from the couch, a strong left hand to the railroad detective's thickly muscled right shoulder.

'Creed,' he said, 'you are a disgusting man! Perhaps the most loathsome of my whole acquaintance! How could you?'

'I had to get it out of him somehow,' Creed replied unhappily.

'He was dying, confound you!'

'And now he's dead,' Creed agreed flatly. 'But I now know what I needed to know.'

'Have you no respect?'

'Plenty, Doctor Sinclair. For you, your daughter – this house; for every good thing everywhere. I did what I felt necessary.' It all sounded rather grand, but Creed did have a continuing guilty doubt as to the purity of his own motives. 'Believe what you like, sir. If there is a God, it's between Him and me.'

'You're a ruffian, Creed!' Sinclair said disdainfully. 'I can't think what your father would have said to that performance. He was a good man.'

'That he was,' Creed acknowledged.

'Kindly leave this house.'

Creed shrugged. It would be pointless to try to justify himself further. He walked to the door, then stepped through into the hall, seeing Lois Sinclair seated on a chair opposite. He realised that she must have heard most of what had passed in the surgery, and showed his hands, shrugging again. The girl rose, her features wooden, and led him towards the front door. This she opened for him, looking towards him at the spot where he had paused. 'Sam,' she said, 'I'm truly sorry.'

'About your father?' he asked in some surprise.

'No,' she said, shaking her head. 'About Madge.'

'Thank you for that, Lois. But it can't be helped.'

'You look – very down.'

'It's been a hell of a day, Lois, what with one thing and another, I'll tell you that.'

'You mustn't be too hard on yourself – or Madge.'

Creed abruptly sensed a much deeper purpose here than he had supposed. 'What is this?' he asked softly.

Lois Sinclair lowered her face, gravely thoughtful. 'I'm not certain how much I should say. I'm far from sure how much of it is my business. I know things you don't know – though even there I'm not certain of how much. And at the end of it is the question as to whether I should actually speak at all.' She looked up quickly, her eyes meeting his. 'Am I making sense, Sam?'

'Not a lot,' Creed said, grinning weakly.

'This does have to do with Madge Stacey?'

'Very much so,' the red-haired girl answered. 'You will be aware that Madge and I were Sunday School teachers at the Wesleyan chapel. Friends–'

'Making all due allowances for the difference in your social positions,' Creed prompted.

'We have a snobbish little town,' Lois Sinclair admitted, sighing. 'If Madge and I weren't friends in the fullest meaning of the word, at least we were women of a similar age and could speak freely to each other. Madge poured out her heart to me the day before she got married. There were confidences I mustn't talk about, but otherwise your name kept coming up all the time, and I had the feeling, that she was hoping that much of what she was telling me would one day reach your ears through me. The truth was that she had no real wish to get married, and had a bit of a grievance against you for blowing hot and cold where she was concerned.'

'But she didn't want to marry Hubert Eichmann? Is that what you're telling me.'

'That's what I'm telling you.'

Creed's brows corrugated, and he stood thinking hard. 'It sounds to me like Madge was having pressure put on her to marry Eichmann.'

'She was.'

'By Eichmann himself or a third party?'

'By Hubert Eichmann.'

'On account of some shortcoming in a third party?'

'I believe so, yes.'

'The third party would have to be somebody close to Madge. Almost certainly a member of her family. She does have a brother and sister, but both are older and married, and neither lives in these parts. That leaves her mother and father.' Creed pulled a face and shook his head. 'I can't see where trouble could arise through either of them, Lois.'

'That's as far as I can go, Sam,' the girl said firmly. 'When I saw how you were thinking earlier on, I didn't want you to end up hating Madge – or yourself.'

'This does put a different complexion on matters,' Creed observed. 'But I am glad it wasn't just me and my ways that sent Madge elsewhere.'

'I'm sure it will be of some consolation to her when she learns that you've finally grown up.'

'Lois, that's taking it a bit far.'

'But is it untrue, Sam?'

'You're seeing with your eyes,' Creed said, 'and I'm seeing with mine. Grown up? I don't feel much different about most things. I still love Madge in a way that only wants what's best for her, and I reckon the kindest thing I can do for her is make my break with the Union Pacific complete. If I don't, there'll come a day when I have to kill Hubert Eichmann – or take him in to face life in jail or the hangman. The young fool is no sooner out of the pen than he's up to his old tricks again, as I learned from Wilf Mansell before he died.'

'You have a problem there, Sam,' the doctor's daughter acknowledged, shaking out the pleats in her lemon-coloured dress. 'Yet only you can decide the course of your own life. You no longer owe a duty of any kind to Madge, but you do owe one to yourself.'

'I should have made the change I planned for today a year ago,' Creed observed, bitterly resentful of his own procrastination now that he could do nothing about it. 'The railroad and I have been uneasy partners for years. I'm too forceful and outspoken, I guess. I've made a share of enemies on U.P. George Binns of this town not among the least.'

'Well,' Lois Sinclair said, heavily judicious, 'for a man who isn't too fond of his employers, you were surely pressing their interests hard with that dying man. Or so it seemed to me.'

'And your father,' Creed growled. 'But, oddly enough, it wasn't so much U.P that I was pushing for. I had the interests of that dying man more closely at heart than you may suppose. I wanted revenge for him, and there could be no revenge unless I knew the salient facts about a big crime that's being planned.' He paused. 'The fact is, Lois, Wilf Mansell saved my life today. Yes, he did – just that. I fell into a bog while I was in the forest, and Wilf fished me out. I do feel I owe that little cuss his revenge on the man who sentenced him to death. Maybe that's why I'm hesitating to turn my back finally on my career as a railroad detective.'

'This Mansell fellow is now dead,' the girl reminded. 'You owe him no more than you owe Madge Stacey.'

'As was,' Creed added ironically.

'What else are you good at, Sam, besides catching thieves?'

'I was going into the cattle business.'

'Not for you. Too slow. Too boring. Too static. Go south,' Lois Sinclair suggested.

'Stick to the law. I read somewhere that they're always looking for the right man to wear a badge down in Arizona. Putting a thousand miles between you and your memories–' There she broke off, stiffening, and a frown settled above her eyes. 'Fiddle-de-dee!'

'What's up?' Creed asked.

'It's Morgan Target,' the girl replied in a quick aside. 'He's coming here, and he looks like thunder!'

'You can bet your boots our esteemed county sheriff is looking for me,' Creed said, bracing himself. 'There'll have been talk about the recent shooting. More trouble!'

FOUR

Creed made to push past the doctor's daughter and leave the house. 'I'd better go outside and speak to the man, Lois,' he said.

'If it is you he wants to talk to, Sam,' the girl said, 'there's no reason why he shouldn't do it in here.'

The county sheriff's huge figure was already looming in the forecourt.

'I don't want to have a quarrel in your father's house,' Creed breathed.

Then the county sheriff's gruff voice said: 'Good evening to you, Miss Sinclair. I'm looking for Sam Creed. A man who knows him told me he saw the fellow come in here.'

'I'm here, Mr Target,' Creed answered from the hall.

'Come in,' Lois Sinclair invited.

Removing his hat, the county sheriff entered the house, frowning at the spot where Creed had retreated into the evening shadows. 'There you are,' he said.

'In the flesh,' Creed agreed. 'What can I do for you?'

Target stepped up to Creed, and the latter felt himself dwarfed, for the county sheriff topped Creed's six-feet two-inches by at least four inches and was otherwise built on the same massive scale. The county lawman was a sardonic individual, with weathered cheeks and brow, a nose of aristocratic proportions, and a thick walrus moustache that obviously enjoyed a regular combing and brushing. For the rest, Target was clad in finely tailored broadcloth, had a waistcoat of flowered silk, complete with gold turnip and chain, and carried an ivory-handled Colt forty-five in a big gunbelt of superbly tooled ox-hide that he wore under his jacket. Target was well known for his shortness of temper, lack of tact, scant respect for any man, and his implacability, all of which appeared to manifest together when he said brusquely: 'Creed, I want you out of Cheyenne by breakfasttime tomorrow. Is that clear?'

'Okay,' Creed said, aware that it would be madness to start arguing with the county sheriff. 'I hear you, Mr Target. It shall be as you wish.'

'You don't ask why.'

'Frankly, I didn't think it would do any good.'

'Perhaps not,' the giant lawman said shortly. 'But I'll tell you nevertheless.' He scowled at Creed's wooden expression. 'You already know why, confound it!'

'Not really,' Creed returned. 'I've committed no crime – unless firing at a bushwhacker rates as one these days.'

'As to that, firing a gun in town does contravene an ordinance,' Target snapped. 'I don't like members of private law concerns – they get above themselves – and that applies especially to the employees of the Pinkerton and Union Pacific agencies.'

'You'd get more satisfaction out of telling head office about that,' Creed commented, offering Lois Sinclair the suspicion of a wink as she stood by, her chin slightly lowered and her palms pressed together, looking faintly embarrassed. 'My orders have always been to co-operate with the real law in every respect. You gave me an order just now, and I've said I'll obey it. I can't do more.'

'Don't get smart!' Target warned, chopping at the air with a huge forefinger. 'I understand a man's hurt.'

'There's one lying dead in the doctor's surgery,' Creed replied. 'I imagine he's still there – and the guys who carried him in.'

'What's his name?'

'Wilfred Mansell. He was one of the old Trevelyan gang.'

'I recall the name,' Target said. 'I'll have a word with the doctor concerning the matter before I leave. So there we have it – a man's dead.'

'Hardly my fault,' Creed said, seeming to have detected a note of accusation in the county sheriff's voice. 'I hope you're not aiming to make that an excuse for something?'

'You seem to admit you're involved,' Target said acutely. 'So firing on the killer wasn't quite done on the spur of the moment?'

'The killer was Les Cable. I had reason to know he was probably around.'

'Had you so? And what was Wilfred Mansell doing in Cheyenne? Perhaps you can tell me that too.'

'He was here to have a drink with me,' Creed explained. 'At the Indian's Head.'

'When did you start guzzling with outlaws, Creed?' the county sheriff demanded. 'I don't like the sound of this. Your name in this town isn't a good one.'

'Wilf Mansell saved my life this afternoon,' Creed replied patiently, going on to provide details of his accident in the forest and what had eventually come out of that – particularly as to the information from the little outlaw concerning the paroled Hubert Eichmann's renewed criminal activities and the reformation of the Trevelyan gang. 'One thing more, Mr Target,' he concluded; 'and I want you to listen to me very carefully. Because this has to do with a major crime that Eichmann and company are planning. The eastbound Flyer is to be stopped by the gang, at Cutman's Pass, on the night of July the eighth. There'll be a large shipment of gold from Sacramento aboard. It seems there's a man named Stanley Barstow also involved. But I'm not sure how he actually comes into it, though I've thought about it hard, and it's possible this Barstow is the go-between for Eichmann and whoever's brain first conceived this job – since I suspect this robbery may have been plotted while Eichmann was still behind bars in the Cañon City prison.'

'This is incredible,' Target said. 'You got all this out of a dyed-in-the-wool villain like Wilfred Mansell?'

'Yes,' Creed answered. 'The details of the big job while he was actually dying. Eich-mann had thrown the poor little varmint out of the gang, and Mansell had run off at the mouth a bit too vengefully about it. That was when Eichmann sent Les Cable out to kill him. There, sir, you know as much about all of it as I do now.'

'Cutman's Pass?' the county sheriff mused.

'That's at the other side of Ganville and towards–'

'I know where it is, Creed, as well as you do.'

'Fine – fine.'

'I've a good mind to lock you up!'

'What's the hate about?' Creed inquired. 'It wouldn't hurt you to be a little bit grateful. I've just done you a lot of good. July the eighth is the day after tomorrow. You have plenty of time to form a posse and hide it at Cutman's Pass to watch out for Eichmann and his crooks. Prevent the robbery taking place, Mr Target, and it will be another feather in your cap.'

'Be that as it may,' the county sheriff said a little huffily. 'It doesn't seem to have occurred to you that your information may not be reliable.'

'I'd stake my life on it.'

'We'll see.'

'Make good and sure that you do,' Creed

warned. 'If you foul up on this, I shan't keep quiet.'

'That's a threat, Creed.'

'Call it what you like,' the railroad detective said evenly. 'So far as I can see, sir, you still haven't told me why I'm being kicked out of Cheyenne.'

'You know very well that you're no longer on the Union Pacific's active list,' came the retort. 'On my reckoning, young man, that means you've been sticking your nose in around here where it isn't wanted.'

'Ah, George Binns has been cackling,' Creed remarked, the light breaking.

'Mr Binns and I had a long talk concerning your presence in town.'

'So you've been minding *my* business, eh?'

'I am the law in Cheyenne,' Target said sternly. 'Everybody's business is my business – when they make it so. Didn't you have thoughts about becoming a rancher?'

'Binns is a weak tap!' Creed seethed. 'Yes, Mr Target, I did have such thoughts, but they may have gone away.'

'Women marry where they please,' Target reminded.

'Binns did a job, didn't he?' Creed reflected. 'I can take it. I'm not going to smash up the town.'

'Do that,' Target grated, 'and you'll never get out of jail. Creed, you're capable of just about anything! Be out of Cheyenne by seven o'clock tomorrow morning. I don't ever want to see your face in this town again!'

'Never was a man to go where he wasn't wanted.'

'Stick to that,' the county sheriff advised, smiling stonily at Lois Sinclair. 'Will you ask your father to give me a few minutes of his time, please?'

'Of course, Mr Target,' the girl said, glancing hesitantly at the railroad detective through the twilight eddying in at the still open front door.

'It's all right, Lois,' Creed said. 'I'll see myself out. Thanks for what you told me. It really is a help.'

The girl nodded, then began leading Morgan Target towards the door to her father's surgery.

Creed stepped outside, shutting the front door behind him, but walked out to the street, smarting a little from the county sheriff's less than fair attitude towards him. He was suddenly sure of what he was going to do next – and in a spirit of defiance too – for he would ride to Ganville and see this matter through, both on Wilfred Mansell's account and for his own satisfaction. This was not something he had to do, or ought to do – since there were many forms of danger in it – but he had come this far, and suffered enough in the process, to regard it as a kind of seal on his career with the Union Pacific. If he had to play a shooting part in whatever came up, so be it; otherwise he would act as an observer and potential back-up. Maybe, too, he wanted to keep an eye on Madge's marriage situation. Better by far, if it could be arranged, that Hubert Eichmann should be returned to prison than suffer a conclusive fate. But all that was in the lap of the gods. Only they knew how it would all come out.

Walking down the street, Creed located his horse. Somebody had been good enough to tie it to a rail for him. Freeing the brute, he led it to the livery barn and put it into lodgings there – leaving the place after that and doing the same for himself at the boarding house run by Mrs Sid Matthews. With his room arranged, he ate at the lady's dining table, then went straight to bed, dropping off to sleep almost at once and remaining unconscious until cockcrow the next morning.

Creed was full of yawns when he left his bed, and he felt far less energetic than he had expected. He realised that he was suffering a reaction to the stresses and strains of the day before, but washed and shaved as a matter of habit, and then went downstairs and ate a breakfast of ham-and-eggs. After that he paid his bill and trudged off to the livery barn, where he collected his horse and fiddled a while over saddling up, for he was more uncertain than ever before – in his lowered state of body and mind – as to whether the course to which he had committed himself so passionately the previous evening was the right one.

Though he knew that this doubt was unquestionably part of his reaction, it seemed to him that he was now tending to weaken in his resolve – perhaps even to lose his nerve – and that made him furious with himself. He could not abide a jibber, and his tendency to back off drove him forward as nothing else could. Less than fully aware of what he was doing, he climbed on his horse and, once outside Cheyenne, let fly with his heels and was soon miles down the trail leading westwards. By degrees, the fresh air got into his brain and sharpened him up, and it began to occur to him that he was still deliberately blocking out common sense and becoming irrational. For what Lois Sinclair had told him was the truth. He owed nothing to anybody just now but himself. He had informed the law of the date and place of the big robbery scheduled by Eichmann and company, and that was all that really mattered. The rest threatened to become a little better than sheer inter-ference, and that could bring penalties of its own. No, he ought to forget this nonsense of riding west to Ganville, go back to Des Moines, and work out a credible future for himself during his next three weeks of furlough. Yesterday – and everything that he had thought and done during yesterday – should be forgotten. There were days in a man's life that should be excised and cast into oblivion. Life, as a newspaperman had once told him, was like writing: the more acceptable for being heavily edited. Yet, knowing – and nobody's fool to boot – he still went on riding westwards. It made a guy despair of himself.

The day began expanding around the trail, and the country ahead – which lay towards Ganville and Laramie – absorbed light and took on colour, while arrows of gold that came flying over his shoulders dissolved into haloes as they entered the mists that clung to the white peaks of the Medicine Row. Keeping his mount to a businesslike pace, Creed stayed vigilant – since there could always be danger around for him in these parts close to the railroad – and thought a time or two of the man into whom he had put lead the previous evening.

He assumed that the wounded Les Cable had covered this ground late yesterday after shooting Wilfred Mansell, and he knew it was unlikely that many travellers – if any – had come this way overnight; so he wondered if there was a chance that he might stumble over Cable's body as he went along; but, as the miles passed by and he saw no trace of a body or loose horse, he was forced to the conclusion that the bushwhacker had either not been as badly hurt as he had thought probable or had left the Cheyenne area by a route other than the present one after all. Anyhow, whatever the hurt or lack of it that he had given Les Cable, it seemed a fair bet that he would encounter the fellow again before everything was done, and he soon let his mind move on to the other matters – chief of which was the question why George Binns, the manager of the railroad depot back at

Cheyenne, should have gone to the trouble of discussing his business in some detail with the county sheriff, Morgan Target. It was clear that something potent enough had been said to get Creed kicked out of town, and he wondered what precisely that could have been. Had sheer dislike been behind it, or was it possible that Binns could have been scared of something said or done? Heaven knew! And it couldn't matter that much now.

The trail rose and fell, never far away from the route followed by the Union Pacific's iron road. It cut through pinewood and leaf forest, skirting rugged slopes and crossing trestle bridges that had been built over deep gorges in which white water boiled. Ahead, dominating the great panorama of Wyoming short of South Pass, loomed more mountain crests – a final glory of ribbed granite and streaming snows – crown, indeed, of a high and lonely world that Creed had wandered at intervals since childhood and where he felt entirely at home. A man who abhorred damage to the natural scene – even to the plucking of flowers – he was just beginning to frown at the inroads which men with axes had lately cut into the tracts of giant cedars that topped what he had been told was the

Territory's oldest forest, when he glimpsed movement where the trail before him tipped downwards through the wide swathe of felled woodland that broke against the not too distant slopes of silver birch and dark erica beneath which he knew the town of Ganville to be situated.

Creed drew rein. Then, hunching forward in his saddle, he peered intently to his front. There was activity below him all right, and he realised that he had come upon Les Cable again sooner than he had expected. But the killer wasn't alone, for he was riding in the company of a man who appeared to be supporting him in his seat by the use of an extended left hand which rested against the deltoid cap of Cable's right shoulder. The sight suggested that the bushwhacker had indeed been quite badly hurt by Creed's shooting of the previous evening; also that Cable would be unlikely to reach medical attention in Ganville without collapsing entirely; and, within moments of the thought registering with the watcher, Cable reeled away to his left and fell sideways out of his saddle. Striking the ground hard, the killer came to rest spine down upon it. He lay motionless for a few seconds, then rolled over onto his elbows and knees and tried to struggle to his feet; but he simply didn't have the power left to make it, and his helper – obviously none too pleased by any of it – was forced to step down and walk round the horses to him. Standing over Cable on arrival, the second man reached down and took a two-handed grip on the fallen shape. Then he jerked Cable erect with the kind of action of which only a very strong man was capable.

Too far away to pick up many details of the second man's dress and appearance, Creed went on considering the pair as a fact of the moment. Though he could not be certain of it, he was reasonably sure that Cable had been operating alone last evening – and that he had left the Cheyenne area in the same fashion – which meant that his helper had either been a companion keeping in the background or somebody who had joined him, in one circumstance or another, during the time since his escape from Cheyenne and a more recent hour. Creed fancied the latter explanation; for, though the two men down there could have been known to each other before this morning, there was little in their general behaviour to suggest the rough comradeship of men working even loosely in tandem. Nor had

Wilf Mansell even hinted at the possibility that he had had a second hunter, and a man of his age and trail-wise sensibilities would have known if such had been the case. No, on the very limited evidence available, it was probable that Cable's helper was just a traveller who had come upon him lying at the wayside – and would offer no resistance if Creed went in and claimed the wounded bushwhacker for the law down in Ganville.

The railroad detective pondered that one for a minute longer. If he kept out of this – and the killer received expert medical help and lived – Cable might well escape into the country over the next day or so and live to commit many a new crime in afteryears. That could hardly be risked, for to arrest the villain now could not possibly constitute any form of interference and must be the right course of action. Inbred to the rest, it would also ensure that Cable *did* get the best doctoring available and be given the chance to survive comfortably – whereas if he were allowed to get away, no matter how carefully patched up, he might well die of wound-neglect out in the wilds and amount to a silent accusation against the watcher at some future date.

Creed kicked at his mount's sides. This

must be done as quickly and smoothly as possible. Down the hill he galloped, his gaze fixed on the two men below, waiting for them to give the first sign that his approach had been detected. The last thing he wanted was to scare Cable's helper into drawing a gun – always assuming the man's innocence of any guilty connection with the bush-whacker – and he prayed that the other would not be foolish enough to let any misunderstanding arise as to what was actually planned here.

It was only then that Creed perceived that his charge downhill was almost certain to provoke a violent reaction of its own accord, and he decided that it would be wise to bring a little discretion to bear and slacken pace while still well short of the pair before him. He could always shout out the nature of his business in the reasonable certainty of getting a verbal reply from Cable's helper. Once the other fully understood the situation, the risk of any shooting ought to be eliminated.

Still a hundred yards from the pair ahead, Creed heaved back on his reins, bringing his horse almost to a halt within the next few moments. Filling his lungs, he opened his mouth to utter a shout, but just then Cable's face came round and a look of shocked fright appeared on his pallid features. 'It's the guy who shot me!' he croaked at his companion. 'Get him, Barstow!'

That name was enough. Creed was instantly sure that the connection between Cable and his helper was not innocent but a close and guilty one. The name Barstow had been one of the imponderables of this affair, and now here he was facing the man.

Barstow, a long-faced, hard-eyed man, with a crooked nose and a scarred right cheek, went for his gun. It was one of the fastest draws that Creed had ever witnessed, and the shot that followed would have hit him squarely had his horse not jinked away from the movement as it occurred. Cable, too, though greatly slowed up by his wound, jerked at his holster, and his right hand also came up flaming, but his bullet flew into the trees on Creed's right and was never a threat.

Straightening the horse and spurring hard, Creed snatched out his own pistol and charged headlong at the two men before him, ignoring the blast of their revolvers and aiming to bowl them over – or at least separate them from their mounts with a finality which would keep them afoot –

then, holding square in his saddle, he aimed his own first shot at Barstow – knowing the unwounded man for by far the more dangerous of his two enemies – and he had the satisfaction of seeing his slug rake across the right side of the other's jawbone and open up a fearful burn from which the blood spilled freely. Screaming with pain, Barstow reeled backwards against Cable's horse; then, revealing himself as no hero, he spun round and forced the animal into a turn, climbing astride it in a following movement with a bounce that was quite remarkable in a man who was really no light weight. After that, maintaining a right hand pressure on the bit, he kept his appropriated horse revolving in the same direction until it faced due north. Now he struck with his rowels and sent the brute arrowing into the clumps of undergrowth left standing by the tree-fellers who had denuded the forest hereabouts; and, by the time the onrushing Creed was within a few yards of the fumbling and knock-kneed Cable, he was almost lost in the obscurity of the further growth and no kind of target worth shooting at. Creed, all too aware of Cable's still flashing Colt, promptly gave all his attention to the man, shooting him through the chest and immediately ending the threat to himself. Then he passed the falling killer, reining in with all the strength of his arms in the process.

Creed's mount skidded to the stand, and he screwed round in his saddle, covering the collapsed Cable with a gun that was cocked and ready; but there was no trace of further aggressive movement from the bushwhacker and he appeared dead. Dismounting, it took Creed only a few moments to ascertain that this was indeed the case, and he stepped back and swore under his breath, for he would now have to take the body into Ganville quite openly and create the kind of stir as to his presence in the area that he had least wanted to make. But it would have to be done, since he could hardly leave a dead man lying in the middle of the trail for the wolves or some old grizzly to chew upon.

Aw, god-dammit! The only good thing about the matter was that he still had Stanley Barstow's horse available as a transport for the corpse; and he was about to dismount and go over to where the animal was standing, when a movement behind a thicket of holly and ivy a short distance down trail of him claimed his full attention and caused him to point a covering gun at the greenery.

Next instant a straight-backed woman came riding out from behind the shrubs. Her presence brought a loud grunt of surprise from Creed, who automatically put up his Colt and said: 'What the hell are you doing here, Madge?'

FIVE

After throwing a glance around him to make certain that they now had this part of the forest entirely to themselves, Creed relaxed and answered the tentative smile on the advancing woman's face with a kind of wary, flinched-off grin of his own. Madge Stacey – or Eichmann as she had recently become – looked good. Her hair, a carefully tended nutbrown mass, cascaded down her neck and on to her shoulders, while the perfect oval of her face contained a pair of shining eyes, a straight nose, and a wide and generous mouth. Her complexion was as flawless as new ivory, and the firmness of her exquisitely shaped body bespoke youth and health – though she had subtly matured since the last time Creed had seen her, and there was just a hint of disillusionment in the way that the skin had tightened at the corners of her mouth and eyes. She was nicely dressed – in a riding habit of coffee velvet, a blouse of cream silk with a neck and cuffs of white lace, a Scottish style bonnet, and tan riding boots – and had obviously gone to some trouble over her appearance. Any man would be proud of her, and Creed had to admit to himself that marriage suited her; though it hurt in some senses that it had been one other than he who had induced these early traces of matronly self-confidence in the ever difficult Madge. 'This is no place for you!' Creed said roughly. 'Have you ever seen a dead man before?'

'Shut up, Sam!' the woman said, halting her buckskin mare a yard or two short of where he sat his own horse.

'Thank you kindly, ma'am.'

'I want to hold you to the point,' Madge responded. 'We may never have another opportunity to talk as privately as this again.'

'Isn't *that* the point?' Creed stressed. 'What *are* you doing here? It *can't* be by accident.'

'It isn't. My husband received a telegram from Cheyenne late yesterday. It informed him that you were in town.'

'Like a good wife,' Creed said ironically, 'you snouted into it.'

'I wouldn't be a friend of yours if I hadn't got a long nose, would I?'

'Guess not.'

'Oh, Sam!' she sighed, shaking her head a trifle despondently. 'What a mess all of it has become!'

'You are married,' he reminded implacably.

'Have I been accused?'

'Didn't mean it like that,' Creed said huffily. 'A girl pleases himself. If she can stomach jailbird, who am I to complain at her taste?'

'Sam, if you have regrets,' Madge said sternly, 'they're your own fault.'

'Sure,' he said sincerely enough. 'I had a talk with Lois Sinclair yesterday evening, and I reckon we just about agreed I'm a selfish, no-account, thoughtless bastard. I had every chance with you. Maybe one or two I didn't deserve.'

'Yes, Sam,' she said levelly. 'I gave you every chance. I would have given you everything. It was you who wouldn't take.'

'That's right,' Creed acknowledged. 'I didn't refuse, Madge – I wouldn't take. There are rules governing these matters. I obeyed them.'

'Yes, you're an honourable man after your fashion,' Madge conceded. 'Even if you do deceive yourself from top to bottom. What you won't risk is responsibility.'

'What hogwash!' Creed exploded, amazed at these reflections on his character. 'Mrs Eichmann, I'd say responsibility is my second name! The Union Pacific have loaded more of it onto my shoulders in the last few years than most men carry in a lifetime.' He scowled. 'Play fair, Madge! I don't send that kind of buckshot whistling round your bustle.'

'I never could talk to you sensibly, Sam!'

'Drop it, Madge!' he advised. 'I've told you once already. You're married. That covers past, present, and future – for you and me. Correct?'

'You're bent on hurting me, aren't you, Sam?'

'All I'm trying to avoid is having to suffer any more hurts myself.'

'What I want you to know is this,' Madge said in measured tones. 'We don't always do what we do because we want to.'

'Lois Sinclair did hint that you were not altogether a free agent in your marriage dealings with Hubert Eichmann,' Creed mused. 'You wanted her to pass that on, didn't you, Madge?'

'Yes. But I was careful to leave it so that you could both only guess at what I really meant.'

'Tell me more,' Creed prompted, adding a sudden and disdainful twist of his lips. 'Or not. It can't change anything. The "till death us do part" bit comes in between.'

'I'm not going into details,' the woman said. 'You must know very well that I can't. If you think hard enough, you may get an inkling. I want you to understand.'

'There's nothing to forgive, Madge.'

'To understand, Sam,' she insisted.

The woman said one thing, but Creed had the feeling that in her inmost heart she wished – or even intended – another; and that riled him up and made him want to chastise her by speaking aloud matters that she wanted only his inner ear to hear. 'It's plain as can be,' Creed said a little brutally, 'that Hubie has a hold on you. I remarked as much to Lois Sinclair. I figured you were protecting somebody close. Well, I have done some thinking. Your papa works for the Union Pacific, doesn't he? Looking back, I'd say he's had spells of living high off the hog that might not bear too much examination. We had a spate of train wrecks a year or two ago.'

'Sam,' Madge begged, 'he had nothing to do with the wrecks.'

'Maybe not,' Creed said narrowly. 'But he

was the overseer on a salvage gang that had the chance to set aside some nice pickings.'

Madge hung her head a trifle, but said nothing.

'I don't care now!' Creed declared contemptuously. 'Let the truth be what it will. I've done with U.P – handed in my notice to quit. It's Samuel Creed Esquire for some new and better way of life. Lois suggested I might go south. They need lawmen in Arizona.'

'Take her with you, Sam.'

'I'm not up to her, Madge,' he said frankly. 'You, perhaps, but not her. Or is it that you wouldn't quite lose me if–?'

'Sam!' she interrupted, blanching with shock. 'Women aren't like that!'

'Oh, yes they are!' he returned bluntly. 'No, honey, we don't quite measure up. We're bolts of a coarser cloth than Lois Sinclair. I've no sure idea of what I'll be doing next, but I'm certain I shan't be romancing the doctor's daughter. No sirree!' He gave his nape a thoughtful scratch, conscious that the subject needed changing, for there were still important details present that had yet to be answered. 'Whose name was signed to that telegram your husband got from Cheyenne?'

'Signed?' Madge shook her head. 'There was just an initial.'

'What was that?'

'B.'

'You don't know who the B stood for?'

'I haven't a clue, Sam.'

'Damn that!'

'It's the truth.'

'There aren't that many folk in your world – or mine.'

'Do you want me to start guessing?'

'If you like.'

'That's crazy!'

'When was comparing ideas ever that?'

'What do I really know of my husband's life?' Madge inquired evasively. 'I've only been married to him a few days!'

'Our lives have revolved about the Union Pacific,' Creed said. 'In a different way, the same goes for his.'

'I rode out from Ganville this morning in the hope of seeing you, Sam,' the woman said. 'I wanted you to understand.'

'I've heard that before, haven't I?' Creed sighed. 'You left Ganville on spec. Well, you and I were always good at guessing each other's mind. And there was just a touch of something to go on, I suppose. If only your vanity.'

'How about yours?'

'Too logical to have any.'

'Really, Sam!'

He inclined his head. 'Your father's name is Bert Stacey. Right?'

'B.'

'The warning that I was back in these parts could have come from him.'

'Or Bill Newman. Or Brian Cole. Or Barney Kellet.'

'Yeah,' Creed conceded, an eyebrow hooking upwards. 'Plenty of B's about, when you come to put your mind to it, eh? The trouble is, they're all railroad men and any one of them could be involved. But how about Binns? We are talking surnames now.'

'George Binns, the depot manager?'

'I don't know of another Binns, do you? He's a man who always knows a sight too much about everything and everybody. Too much time on his hands, I'd say.'

'You've never trusted him.'

'Not for a minute.'

'But what you said a few moments ago covers for him too,' Madge reminded. 'I trust him, Sam. George is all right. The men at the depot could have a lot worse boss than he. And, Sam – you've got pretty close, at this time and that, to accusing him of – of things, you know.'

'That's something else I can't deny,' Creed admitted. 'Where mistrust is, no loving relationship can be, eh?' He smiled tightly, then fixed what amounted to a shot in the dark. 'What can you tell me about Stanley Barstow?'

There was a small catch in Madge's breath, and she looked uncomfortable to the point of being shifty. 'How does he come into this?' she blurted.

'I have inside information,' Creed responded. 'I've learned there's a bullion theft due off one of the Flyers. Stanley Barstow has some part in it. So does your husband – and the rest of the boys who used to ride with Norm Trevelyan.' He sucked his teeth, letting a frown build. 'What matters, Madge, is that the guy's known to you. He was here before you showed yourself, wasn't he?'

'I saw him from hiding, yes – before he fled,' Madge acknowledged. 'I had to keep out of the way, Sam. You seem to know an awful lot more than you ought to – for a man who's spent so much time in Des Moines of late. Are you sure you've tilted up with the Union Pacific? You're behaving too much like your old self to be anything but a railroad detective.'

'I won't fence with you any more, Madge,' Creed said shortly. 'I'm not really here today for anybody's advantage but yours. Yes, you may find it hard to credit, but that's the truth. I'd rather see your husband back in jail for a reasonable term than hanged or locked up there for life. You must know as well as I do that he's headed for something extreme.' Leaning forward, he gave his restive mount a soothing pat on the right shoulder. 'Okay, dammit! I won't play the hypocrite! I'd be happy to see Hubie dangling or locked away for good; but I know you'd come out as the loyal wife and it would break your heart. I don't want to see your life ruined before it's started. If I can help the law see that doesn't happen, I'll leave these parts a happier man than I would have done before.' He paused, only just keeping the plea out of his eyes. 'Can you help me to help you, Madge?'

'You make it sound so reasonable!' the woman protested. 'If I say one word, whether by accident or design, that helps put Hubert back in prison, he'll never forgive me. But, if I don't help you to help me – assuming I'm able – and he ends up dead or behind bars again, I'll never forgive myself. Is that a conflict of loyalties or being hoist by the horns of a dilemma? What do you think, Sam?'

'You want it easy!' he accused.

'I want it possible!' she flashed back.

'No matter what difficulties you may think you see right now,' Creed insisted, 'no real harm has yet been done and everything is still possible. Whatever happens today will probably look like something quite different five years from—'

A yell went up a fair distance away. Creed raised his eyes towards the sound, while Madge twisted round in her saddle and peered behind her with the same purpose. Creed made out a body of horsemen about a quarter of a mile beyond them. 'It's my husband and those friends of his!' Madge announced. 'They must have come looking for me!'

'Hubert may have sensed you were up to something,' Creed reflected. 'He's as quick on the uptake as you or I.'

'I – I must go to him,' Madge said hesitantly. 'He is my—'

'He is your husband!' Creed interrupted bitterly. 'Do we have to keep repeating it?'

The woman fetched her horse round. Gigging up, she began riding towards the oncoming horsemen. A rifle banged at the forefront of the party, and the bullet hit the trail on Madge's right, whining. Then a second shot plucked visibly at her bonnet, while a third whipped at her skirt, just touching flesh, and she let out a quick cry of pain.

Creed couldn't believe it. 'That's Eichmann!' he cried. 'The skunk is shooting at you!'

'He can see it's you!' Madge declared, glancing back in horror.

'Come on – and to hell with him!' Creed roared, spurring savagely and swerving at the female, his left hand reaching out and yanking her mount's head round from the bit. 'You can go back to his loving embrace later on – when he's cooled off some!'

'Loving embrace!' she cried through her teeth, picking up her companion's intention and slapping her horse along in the right direction. 'The louse!'

They headed northwards, galloping hard as they zigged and zagged among the stumps of the great trees which the loggers had lately felled. The odd shot pursued them, but the bullets were flying wide now, and they soon cleared the swathe of land which had been denuded of trees and entered the far larger expanses of uncut woodland beyond. Here they drubbed through mighty halls of cedar which reached before them into backdrops of shade and silence, while the ground eventually rose ahead of the stretching horses into outcropping granite that burst out of yellow clay and finally pushed above the treetops themselves, bringing the riders out against the aching brightness of the summer sky and into cool airs which had crossed mountain ice not so long ago. Noting that the horses were all of a sweat at this stage and blowing hard, Creed raised a staying hand and reined in, looking back at the same moment. 'Can't see anything of them,' he said; but then he couldn't see much at all in the gloom beneath the green ceiling of the forest.

'Did they turn after us?' Madge wondered.

'I'm not even sure about that,' Creed confessed. 'What would you have done in their place?'

'Pursued.'

'That's how I read it too,' Creed acknowledged. 'But following us won't be easy. I don't see them getting far with it.'

'It's a nose with Hubert rather than an eye,' the woman commented uncertainly. 'Instinct, I suppose.'

'He's good at tracking folk?'

'So his friends say. He's got a heap of confidence in himself.'

'Well, we can't just keep this up willy nilly.'

'Why not?' Madge asked tightly. 'I'm game.'

'Are you bleeding much?'

'It's just a nick on the side of my thigh,' she said dismissively, inspecting the fairly big bloodstain which had ruined her skirt. 'He was shooting to harm.'

'The hellion was shooting to kill,' Creed gritted. 'He's got a vile temper on him. It sure was a bit of a facer, him coming on us like that. Our luck's plainly not such that we should take too many chances.'

'I suppose you feel there's too much left undone around here?'

'Madge,' Creed said seriously, 'if you and I kept riding – though it might be innocent enough in itself – we'd give that husband of yours an excuse to hunt us relentlessly. I can't, and won't subject you to that; and that's not an excuse, so don't you think it.'

'Even if I did,' the woman answered. 'I wouldn't blame you for it. I came looking.'

'You left Ganville on spec,' Creed reminded. 'You could far more easily have been wrong in that than right. I'd have drifted this way all right, but maybe not today. The issue was kind of settled for me yesterday evening when Morgan Target ordered me out of Cheyenne.'

'What had you done?' Madge asked in some surprise. 'There seems to be a bigger story surrounding you than I have yet heard.'

'There was a bushwhacking in Cheyenne last evening.' Creed explained. 'I was sort of involved. That fellow Cable – the guy I killed back there – plugged Wilfred Mansell, a one-time comrade of your husband's. It's a murder I blame on Hubert, Mrs Eichmann, though it might take a bit of proving. But leaving all that aside, and to be quite honest about it, I think I got ordered out of Cheyenne because George Binns had been speaking about me behind my back. He's always had the county sheriff's ear. They're two varmints who figure they were born with the right to sit in judgment on the rest of us.'

'I feel there's so much missing, Sam. I'd truly like to hear all your story since you returned to Cheyenne.'

'I came back from Des Moines with the intention of asking you to marry me,' Creed said. 'I'd put a wad of money together, and

I figured we could set up in ranching. Poor notion, maybe. I got talking to George Binns about it, and he was pleased to be able to tell me that you had recently married Hubert Eichmann. My reaction was about what you'd expect, and I reckon Binns' trouble-making came out of that. Anyway, this is no place to be storytelling. The great outdoors is fine, Madge, but you need a hearth and armchair for yarning.'

'I know of a place where we can go, Sam. We should be safe there until we can sort ourselves out.'

'Where's that?'

'You'll see,' Madge responded, jerking round in her saddle and showing a renewal of fright as an angry male voice echoed up to them through the treetops at their back. 'That's Hubert again!'

'Rot his guts!' Creed seethed. 'How in tarnation did he latch onto us down there?'

'Does it matter?' the girl demanded, heeling at her mount and passing through a jagged notch in the reef of capstone to their left.

Pulling at his mount's head, Creed followed Madge off the high place and downwards. Soil soon covered the outcropping granite again and grass grew as an ever thickening presence on the slope beneath them. Then they came to the treetops once more, a stiff breeze tossing at the green spires intermittently and bringing forth all manner of creaks and groans from the aromatic boughs below. Gazing at his companion's back, as they plunged into the timber, Creed had the feeling that Madge knew exactly what she was about, and he was content to stay in her tracks as their rapid swaybacked descent carried them down onto broad levels of undergrowth and shadow. Here the bottom of the woods became visible again, and a path westwards – probably an old Indian trail – showed itself, deep-cut and flint-studded, in the gloom a snaking presence that soon curved round towards the back of Ganville. Moving onto the track, Madge stirred her horse to another effort, and Creed was now certain that she knew precisely where she was headed. Uneasy still, however, he looked back over his right shoulder and through the empty forest in their wake, seeking any trace of their hunters, but Eichmann and company were nowhere in sight, and he grew confident that they had indeed been pursuing more by luck than judgment. He had, too, rather feared that Madge's unknown destination, apparently so definite, might be known to her husband also – and suspected because of it – but that did not seem to be the case either. It was all a matter of being thankful for small mercies.

Once more they started climbing at a steep angle. The horses began to sweat and struggle again, tucking deeply at the haunches and gasping with effort. Creed imagined that the ascent through the timber would prove moderately short and direct, but then more of the out-cropping granite intervened and forced them into the checks and hesitations of a naturally staggered course, and several minutes of frustration resulted before they came to the top of the path and passed on to a brush-clad terrace that had a bow of vertical cliffs at its back, a final step to the raw stone of the mountain scene now looming in the background.

The woman led Creed into the shadows of a considerable thicket. Here, by tacit agreement, they drew rein, allowing their horses to snort and blow during a minute or two of much-needed rest. Relaxing themselves, they looked back across the timbertops that filled the valley which they had just crossed, and Creed picked out the ridge from which they had commenced their traverse, at once spotting riders halted on the high spot opposite who were hunched in animated talk with a horseman who sat his mount separately and somewhat to the left of the cluster.

'It's them!' Madge said excitedly. 'Can they see us over here?'

'I don't think they've any idea of where we are,' Creed said, voice narrowing to suit the condition of his eyes, and he reached into a saddlebag and extracted a pair of field-glasses. 'I'm not sure they ever had much.' Putting the glasses to his eyes, he made a quick but delicate adjustment to the focusing wheel. 'Yes, I thought so. That's Stanley Barstow over there. What's he telling Eichmann and that bad bunch of his?'

It was, of course, impossible to get any satisfactory clue as to what was being said over there – about a mile away – and Creed could only frown to himself and examine the possible answers cast up by his own mind. That Barstow had earlier in the day found the now dead Les Cable lying at the wayside could be in little doubt, and it was likely that Barstow – already suspected by Creed of being a go-between since he had never been a known member of the

Trevelyan gang in the past – had been carrying a message between Cheyene and Ganville at the time he was found. So, accepting that a message was involved, it would almost certainly have been sent to Hubert Eichmann, and it was probable that it was being delivered and discussed right now. Creed could be certain of nothing here, but the pieces fitted neatly enough, and he had a strong instinctive feeling that his reasoning could be trusted in this.

But then the distant horsemen did something that surprised and, in a curiously aggravating way, almost affronted him. For, appearing to dismiss their recent chase as no longer having any significance with them, they turned back off the ridge to their right and filed downwards after Eichmann, bound on what errand Creed could not determine – but clearly one that the gang-boss now regarded as being far more important than hunting down his perhaps unfaithful wife.

SIX

Creed put his field-glasses back in the saddlebag. Then he turned his face to Madge and said: 'You didn't tell me what you know about Stanley Barstow. Are you going to?'

'I don't know much,' the woman replied. 'I actually met him for the first time when he called at my mother-in-law's house last Sunday. Hubert and he are friends. I gathered that Barstow used to visit my husband while he was in Cañon City prison. Apart from that, I'd seen him round Cheyenne a few times.'

'Doing what?'

She shook her head.

'Ever see him around the depot?'

'Once. Many other people too. Like you – lots of times.'

'Did you, by any chance, happen to see him speaking with George Binns?'

'No.'

Creed sighed. 'No help.'

'Are you trying to convince yourself

George Binns is the villain of the piece, Sam?'

'I'm coming to the opinion somebody like him has to be responsible,' Creed said. 'Too much railroad crime has centred on Cheyenne in recent years. There could well be somebody in management – somebody who knows all that's going on in other words – who's picking off the plums. Those train wrecks of not so long ago were all packed with goodies. Selected. Now there's this bullion business due the night after next– It could be George Binns, you know.'

'But you haven't a shred of proof, Sam!' Madge declared. 'It's all prejudice!' There was a long pause during which their eyes held. 'Sam, you do know what the word means?'

'Sure.'

'It's judgment based on dislike or untrustworthy evidence.'

'Have you no shame?'

'Not much.'

'I don't believe you have either,' Madge said stiffly. 'These horses have had a good blow. Let's be on our way.'

'Yes, ma'am.'

'You're impossible!' she announced, knee-ing her horse out of the shadows and leading onwards again, the weight of her hand at the bit taking them round to the right and towards the southern end of the cliffs at the back of the terrace. 'You haven't changed in the slightest!'

'The pity of it is,' Creed said, as he followed on, 'we no longer have the chance to find out.'

Madge didn't even bother to turn her head. His words had obviously been beneath her notice. She had said her say on the subject. Back straight as ever, she guided her horse through the tangles of scrub oak, firbrush, mountain ash and briars which made up the thickets of the wide ledge that they were crossing. Nothing hindered, they reached the mighty angle of rock for which the woman had been heading, rounded it on a shelf of stone that was part of the terrace proper, then came to a gully on the left. This sunken feature was choked to the brim with scree and detritus, and they rode across the top of the blockage itself, coming to a vast hillside and another considerable tract of forest.

Creed saw a path before them here. They pursued it southwards and then down into the middle pine slopes, which eventually descended to their limit above the rooftops of Ganville. The scene was remote and impressive without being in any sense lonely. Then, where the path entered an idyllic clearing, they rode up to a side door in a recently built log cabin of unusual size and luxurious design. It had red chimney-pots, windows of leaded glass, and an oaken verandah that had been raised on thick stilts across the steeply falling ground at its front. This verandah was roofed with slates, protected by carved railings, and fitted with leather-topped seats. It also offered a panoramic view of the town below and the wooded country towards Cheyenne. 'Some place!' Creed observed, dismounting in imitation of his companion's latest action. 'Whose is it?'

'Mine,' Madge answered, not without a certain pride. 'It's the home that Hubert had built for him and me to share.'

'That cuss was pretty sure of himself all right,' Creed commented. 'It's not some shack that was put up in a day. No, sirree-bub!'

'I'm glad you like it, Sam.'

'I can separate the man from his deed in this,' Creed admitted.

The woman reached down a key from a hiding place above the door and unlocked the cabin. 'Come in,' she said. 'We should be safe up here for a while. There's no easy way of approaching this spot, so visitors are few.'

'Mixed blessing,' Creed remarked, entering the new dwelling at the female's heels. 'Nor so good when it comes to the toting.'

'I've only seen the good part as yet.'

'Of your marriage?' Creed wondered ironically, staring pointedly at the spot where a little blood still welled through her skirt. 'You'd better fix that leg, hadn't you?'

'I guess so,' she returned indifferently, smiling round at him as they passed out of the kitchen and into the drawing room, which had a floor made of oaken blocks that was carpeted with furs, a fine couch and upholstered armchairs, a shingled fireplace – above which a splendid set of moose antlers had been fixed – and a good variety of unexpectedly tasteful ornaments and paintings, items that had no doubt been shipped in from back East. 'I shan't die of it. Nice, isn't it?'

The question obviously referred to the furnishings and general design of the room. 'It already shows a woman's touch,' Creed conceded. 'Yeah, it's real nice.'

'That would be Hubert's mother,' Madge

admitted. 'She's a woman of taste. But Hubert has given me a free hand. I can make any changes I wish.'

'Well, I wish you joy of it,' Creed said a mite unhappily. 'It's not every newly wed girl gets a start like this one, Madge.'

'Or even ends up with a place like this?' the girl queried. 'I'll go into my bedroom and fix this leg. Make a change of clothing too. You have a look round. I'll be back with you as soon as I can.'

'Take your time over it.' Creed advised, nodding. 'There's plenty here to keep a man interested – so take your time.'

The woman left the room through a door in the back of the wall on the further side of the fireplace, and the catch clicked behind her.

Left to himself, Creed went first to the front window of the room and gazed out upon the world of light and colour that fled into far and rocky distances beyond the verandah – envying a little yet only in so far as he could never have given Madge anything this good – and then ceasing all envy as he remembered that what he found here had almost certainly been purchased with stolen money. Eichmann was at best a thief, at worst a murderer, and one who would surely go unrepentant to his grave. There was nothing about Hubert Eichmann that any honest man should envy. Except, perhaps, his wife; but even she had probably come to him via a dishonest ploy.

Creed turned his mind away from these thoughts. Even if Eichmann had acquired his wife by threatening to expose her father as a thief like himself, the union had been blessed and consummated, and must last until death dissolved it. So again made restless by it all, the railroad detective sauntered back into the kitchen and then to the further side of the cabin, unbolting a door there and stepping out into the back yard.

Glancing round again, he saw that this space was no less well appointed than the rest of the property. It had two strongly built sheds, a stable big enough to house three or four horses, and a brick privy that was placed not too far from the back door. His tread remaining slow and lazy, Creed walked over to the nearer of the sheds and, his curiosity frank and unashamed, opened the door and peered inside, seeing that a chopping block, axes, and a number of gardening tools were stored inside. He grunted his approval, admiring how every need of the new household had been foreseen and met with the best that could be had from a town like Ganville. Then, with the first shed closed up again, he moved on to the second, attempting to open that too; but he found a lock against him here, and it seemed altogether too big and strong to meet the security requirements of an outhouse.

Normally, used to the more haphazard planning of the average household – which was usually dictated by availability anyway – Creed would have taken little notice of this detail, but everything else ordered by Eichmann had so exactly matched its need that he wondered why the second shed should be so heavily secured; and, going round to the back of the erection, he raised himself on tiptoe and looked in through the window there, seeing at once – against the red planking of the wall on his right – a pile of boxes, which was covered by a blanket across the top and only visible as grey and sinister-looking along a strip of the front that was visible just above the ground. The colouring was the giveaway to a man of Creed's experience, for grey paint was only used on boxes that contained dynamite.

Lowering himself off tiptoe, Creed stroked his jaw and pondered the matter. It wasn't that he was the least bit surprised to find high explosives on the premises – for dynamite no doubt had its occasional place in Eichmann's lawless plans – but the quantity here was considerable and probably no more than a temporary provision; for no man in his right mind would make a habit of keeping enough dynamite to blow his home sky-high within a few paces of his back door. So this pile of high explosives, on a reasonable judgment, was most likely that to be used to create a blockage on the railroad track somewhere along Cutman's Pass. Therefore, if he could break into the shed and spoil the dynamite yonder by removing it from its boxes and dumping it in the rainwater that filled the butt near the back door, he could probably eliminate any final risk that damage might be produced on the ironroad some miles west of here. Indeed, he was still enough of a Union Pacific man to feel that keeping the company's services running, by avoidance of all forms of disruption, was as vital to the general good as catching criminals or spotting where damage could occur along the way.

Returning to the first shed, Creed opened its door again and stepped inside, glancing over the tools present and wondering with which he could do the fastest job of breaking open the second shed. He had settled on a heavy logging axe, when it occurred to him that he had a pistol in his holster which had the power to shatter a lock with no more effort than it took to pull the trigger. This appeared to be his best answer, and he was getting ready to once more retrace his steps, when it crossed his mind that it might yet prove unnecessary to employ any form of violence on the lock that stood between him and the dynamite, for Madge could well have the keys in use about the property with her indoors.

Deciding that it could do no harm to ask her about it anyway, Creed faced away from the sheds and made to re-enter the cabin; but he had yet to pass inside when he heard horses approaching through the pines to the west of the dwelling. The voices of young men were audible too, and their calling became louder by the moment, a reckless vein of devil-may-care delight emanating from the coarse things they shouted at each other.

Creed checked. He was as sure as made no difference that the oncoming riders were Hubert Eichmann and fellow badmen. This was the worst kind of development – and his mind raced. He must do the best he could for both Madge and himself and, to that end, it seemed wisest that he dart through the cabin, grab his horse at the other door, then spring on it and ride back into the trees on the opposite side of the dwelling before any of the newcomers had the chance to spot him. When all was said and done, Madge was Eichmann's newly wedded wife and he ought to be feeling a little more gentle towards her by now. Yet, sooner or later, she would still have to face him in the light of the day's earlier events. Hubert would no doubt bawl her out, and might even kick her backside, but he would be unlikely to kill her if she seemed to be alone up here and he could believe that she had abandoned him. Creed, somewhere out in the limberlost and was now penitent for having offended her spouse. On top of all that, he should not underestimate Madge and her own powers of invention. She would probably be able to take in the lately besotted Hubert quite easily.

Literally flinging open the back door, Creed plunged into the loghouse at top speed – and things instantly began to go wrong. For he charged into Madge, who entered the kitchen rather suddenly from the drawing room adjacent and they both went flying. Creed fell sprawling in the middle of the floor, while the woman staggered away from the impact and struck the wall opposite, cannoning off to lurch back into the room and catch herself two-handed on the top of the kitchen table. 'What are you doing, Sam?' she demanded hotly.

He picked himself up, badly shaken. 'Horsemen coming!'

She straightened her body, throwing a hand to her throat. 'Hubert?'

'I think so.'

'No! Which way?'

He jerked a thumb over his shoulder, indicating the back yard.

She nodded abruptly, appearing to understand now what he had been trying to do, and she faced round and said: 'Go!'

Opening the door beyond Madge, he went, eyes darting about him as he entered the open, and he saw that his horse – left unsecured – had wandered over to a patch of grass several yards away and was literally plucking the blades out of the dry soil. 'Blast you!' he gritted unreasonably, going for the brute at a crouched run and almost propelling himself into the saddle.

Filling leather, he reached forward and swept up his reins, already spurring to the front. Then, loosely seated and looking everywhere but in the direction that he was riding, it came as a spine-jarring shock to him when another animal collided head on with his own and the force of the impact shot him backwards out of the saddle and into a fall that brought him down on his buttocks, elbows flat to the ground and raised knees spread wide apart.

Stunned, Creed could not get a full grasp on what had happened; but then he saw another man sprawling on the ground beyond him in much the same position as himself; and he realised that, just as he had been moving in one direction without due care, so had the newcomer been doing the same from the opposite. The other must in fact have come galloping blindly round the northern end of the cabin without a thought in mind but reaching the door out of which Creed had lately emerged; and the railroad detective supposed that his fellow sufferer in the collision – riding out of the forest on the western side of the cabin – must have spotted some form of movement in the new dwelling through the kitchen window and promptly galloped round the walls of the building to make an interception. Now they could only lie back on their elbows and glare at each other; though it seemed to Creed that the newcomer's wits must have unscrambled first, for the neatly moustachioed young man yelled: 'It's you!'

'Yeah, Eichmann,' Creed agreed thickly, 'it's me!'

'Curse you for a polecat!' Eichmann screeched, tipping onto his left side and jerking at the weapon in his holster.

Creed made a similar movement, but was still dazed and missed the butt of his revolver altogether. He feared it was a done job, as the muzzle of the gun opposite seemed to yawn in his face; but in the same instant one of the horses involved in the accident staggered between the two men on the ground and Eichmann could only swear in frustration as he lost his target amidst kicking equine legs. Terror clearing his senses as nothing else could, Creed sprang to his feet and lurched at Eichmann as the intervening horse continued its crazy dance to the left. His right boot kicking, Creed's toe made contact with the young villain's Colt and tore it from his grasp. After that, in passing, he brought down his right fist on Eichmann's crown, striking the same kind of blow that he might have done with a mallet, and the crook flattened against the earth and lay writhing dazedly.

Throwing desperate glances around him as he sought his horse, Creed realised that neither his own mount nor the one which had just saved him – which he now saw to be Eichmann's – was close enough by to attempt catching in the present crisis; for he could hear Eichmann's followers calling out from just beyond the northern end of the cabin and knew that they were about to round it in the same reckless manner as their leader had done. He promptly ran to the right, heading for the trees on that hand, but had yet to reach them when hurrahing horsemen cut a fast curve across his path and forced him to dodge back in the reverse direction.

Men kicked and lashed at him, and a gun went off. Mounts surged and broke, a gap appearing between the head of one and the rump of another, and through the space Creed darted, forcing his stumbling run into better disciplined strides, and up the hill beyond the cabin he ran and into the trees. Through fir and broad leaves he dashed, ripped at by underlying briars and brambles – skin lacerating and garments tearing – weak of limb but ever clearer in the head, and soon he was fully himself again and thinking constructively about the mess he was in, for he could hear Eichmann's riders bursting through the underbrush at his back now and the voice of their more distant leader egging them on.

Dashing sweat from his eyes, Creed attempted to vary his straight ascent by angling sharply to his right, but he had not covered many yards when he found himself at the edge of a sheer drop and had to scuttle back to his left – trying a similar tactic there – but here again, with a dozen paces covered, he came to another precipice and only just caught himself on the brink: teetering there and looking down a couple of hundred feet into a gully where mountain waters rushed and boiled, white caps swirling about the black rocks which jutted wetly along the dark edges of the undulating flow.

It occurred to Creed that he was trapped. In his ignorance of the terrain, he had trapped himself. Misled by the abundant presence of trees and bushes, he had set himself to climb a relatively narrow spur of rock and earth that he had believed to be a hillside, and the facts that he had just discovered about the formation warned him now that, cut off as he was behind, he could only go onwards and up until such time as he ran out of ground and found himself isolated against the sky.

Thus he had few options – and knew himself at mortal risk – but the instinct to survive drove him back into motion and mindlessly upwards. He continued his lung-bursting dash uphill through more symptoms of fatigue, legs tightening to the degree that cramp must seize them soon and his heart threatening to stutter into arrest as he willed one last effort out of himself time after time – like some glutton for punishment trying to stuff himself with suffering.

Now the trees and hanging foliage broke, and the summit of the spur reared into view, bald of all save lime-scoured grasses. Clearing the last of the greenery, Creed staggered upwards to the highest point. Here he turned at bay, with the chasm of the fast waters plunging on his right, a drop of two or three hundred feet at his back, and the same on his left. A fugitive without much hope, he drew and cocked his revolver – determined to make a real fight of it – but his pursuers were not quite stupid and, with him an open target above them, hung back in the fringe of greenery below and fired at him from what amounted to concealed positions.

His perch laced by slugs, Creed shot back at moving targets half-seen, and he had already emptied his Colt when the inevitable occurred. A bullet burned across the upper left side of his body, slapping with great force, and the violence of it spun him off his pinnacle. Then he was in space and falling – falling between the black walls of the deep cutting with the torrent flooding through its bottom.

SEVEN

This had to be it. Creed believed survival out of the question. If the rocks below didn't smash out his brains, the rushing waters would certainly drown him. Well, it all had to end somewhere and he supposed that he could have met a worse death. He just hoped that he wouldn't know too much about it when he snuffed out. No man wished to suffer more than—

His fall ended as he struck water. Down he went and deep. The cold abruptly chilled his sweating body through. And a form of horror possessed him. There was no light, just a tumble of glazed shadows that closed in upon him and threatened to form an insubstantial prison. Knowing that he couldn't last long at the bottom of the cutting, Creed tried to break the drowning grip of the water's conflicting currents and swim upwards while there was still some buoyancy left in him, but the striking bullet had largely paralysed his left side and he could do no more than flounder awkwardly while toppling over and over like a submerged log. More scared of fear itself than being afraid, Creed got a firm grip on his mind. It seemed that his hope of a quick death was not to be fulfilled. That being so, he would just have to drown as bravely as he could.

But it seemed a day when the unexpected ruled, for the torrent suddenly rushed into some shallows and he was more or less propelled to the surface. It was like a blessed miracle, and Creed began to gulp and gasp at once in the cutting's sweet airs, rapidly recovering his breath. Within moments, however, the torrent began to deepen again and he started spinning once more as the unseen forces in the depths renewed their strength. Fearing that he would soon be in trouble again, Creed made an effort to grab at the rocks that bordered the channel on his left and pull himself to at least temporary safety on that jagged shoreline; but he was neither long enough in the arms nor sufficiently mobile to manage that and he might soon have begun to sink again if conditions had got as bad as before. As it was, the flow remained swift but mostly gentle and he found no difficulty in staying afloat. Presently the waters cornered and, at the other side of the bend, the channel widened considerably and the walls that enclosed it quickly settled to no more than thirty feet in height. Now plenty of light reached the surface of the mountain drain, and summer filled the sky again.

Things got better and better after that. Its volume now broadly spread, the flood became a stream in which the wounded Creed could swim without difficulty, and a rising floor soon caused it to run fleet and reach a bank of sand and pebbles. Plugged by barely submerged hoofprints, this feature was obviously used as a ford and here, going to the left, Creed rose up and walked ashore. Now he checked, bleeding and bedraggled, and looked up at the path which slanted back through the cliff adjacent and provided a way into the forest that covered the land above. Considering the lie of the land, Creed judged that the trail which crossed the water here would have been the one by which Hubert Eichmann and his party had approached the newly built cabin that could not be too far beyond this spot in the woods on the higher ground. Not seeing what else he could do – for he was lost without his horse and must try to recover it from Eichmann's property –

Creed made for the path that fell back through the cliff before him and started to climb, reaching the top about a minute later and literally dropping onto his backside behind a large trailside cedar that provided plenty of shade and the sweet scent of its wood to soothe him in his sudden fatigue.

Silently thanking heaven that he was still alive, he let the side of his head rest against the cedar's gnarled trunk while he examined his wound. It was in fact no worse than a long, deepish groove which started above his floating ribs and travelled diagonally upwards to terminate at a spot behind and just below the left armpit. The injury hurt like fury, and was weeping blood and water at intervals down its whole length, but it was in no sense incapacitating as yet, and he reckoned that, so long as he didn't get an infection into it, he would be able to go on much as usual until it healed. True, it needed binding up, but that – depending on what he found at Eichmann's cabin, when he got there again – might be done by Madge, or even himself, if he could somehow steal the necessary cloth for a bandage.

It would have been oh so easy just then to sit nursing his wound and go to sleep; but he felt a strong compulsion to get on with it, and he was in the act of scrambling up and turning towards the trail that passed the other side of the cedar tree, when he heard horses moving in his direction from further along the track to the east. Immediately stopping his larger movements, he settled back against the mighty bole behind him, relying on the great mass of the cedar's body to hide his presence from the approaching riders.

There he stood, absolutely motionless, and the horsemen – Eichmann and company, as he had expected and now managed to ascertain from the tail of his eye – rode quite slowly past a minute or so later. All exuberance had now drained from the young men, and their talk and manner had become much more sober. Well, so far as they were concerned, a man had recently died at their hands, and it would be remarkable if they were so inhuman that another's murder had had no restraining effect on their spirits. But doubtless they were the scum of the earth nevertheless.

Once the riders were well beyond him – at the top of the descent to the ford in fact – Creed twisted his head to the right and peeped out after them. They numbered six, inclusive of their leader, and were carrying grey boxes upon their saddles that he recognised as those which he had seen through the window of Eichmann's locked second shed. He nodded to himself in satisfaction at the sight, for it hardly required genius to work out that the bad-men were almost certainly in process of carrying dynamite to Cutman's Pass. Creed judged it early for the gang to be setting high explosives against the needs of their projected robbery, but youth was keen and the young crooks were probably spending their ill-gotten gains – if only in their own minds – far ahead of the actual event. They had yet to learn the meaning of the words 'Man proposes, God disposes'. Well, he was on the side of the angels in this, and he knew that he could depend on Morgan Target – for all the county sheriff's bull-headedness and bullying ways – to be worth a whole cohort of the heavenly host come darkness tomorrow, the night of July eighth.

Something stirred significantly in Creed's brain; then died just as suddenly. But, as he left the back of the cedar tree – with the riders completely vanished from up here and gone down towards the lower level of the ford – he felt a question mark branded where the stirring had been. He struggled hard to resurrect whatever glimmering had touched his imagination just now, as he resumed walking eastwards along the trail, but he had no mental energy left at that time, and his subconscious was still unrequited when, about ten minutes later, he saw the red chimney-pots of Hubert Eichmann's fancy loghouse peeping through the branches of the trees ahead of him.

The sight did nothing to energise him, in mind or body, and he tiredly plodded every step over that last one hundred yards or more, wondering now what he was about to find at the cabin – if anything at all; for, though some fairly dramatic events must have occurred there just recently, the place could now be emptied out completely at Eichmann's wish – and he crossed the back yard and went up to the kitchen door. Putting out a hand to open it, though he rather expected the woodwork to be bolted fast again, he was quite pleasantly surprised as the knob turned in his hand and the door swung inwards at his lightest touch, letting him back into the room from which he had fled in such haste well over an hour ago.

Creed was at once conscious of the disturbed atmosphere in the dwelling. He checked instantly and, only a single pace beyond the threshold, bated his breath and listened intently, at once picking up a sound of female sobbing from the drawing room. 'Madge!' he called quite loudly, wishing to reduce the shock that she was probably going to experience at his return.

There was a startled pause, and the crying ceased. Then there was a rush of movement out of the adjoining room and the woman appeared in the doorway to his right and at the further side of the kitchen. The colour was newly drained from her face, and her eyes were big with a vaguely frightened surprise, but she was otherwise a mess too, for she had been hit by a fist which had split her lips and nostrils, and the bruising from the blow had already extended to the inner corners of her eyes and given her, temporarily, the dusky appearance of a white person with coloured blood. 'The bastard!' Creed seethed, his fists opening and shutting in an extreme of suppressed violence. 'How could he bust you up like that?'

'I suppose I was somewhat at fault,' Madge snuffled.

'Never!' Creed declared. 'There's no excuse for what he's done. That settles it! I'm going to bring him in myself – and if he gets killed in the process, too bad!'

'They – they,' she breathed, 'they said–'

'I can well imagine what those clowns said,' Creed ground out. 'It's no goodness of theirs that I'm still alive! I ought to be dead, Madge, how I fell into the torrent. I'd never get the same breaks again in a thousand repeats. Even the g'damned bullet cut me open without doing any serious harm. Hell, girl! How lucky can a man get?'

'It looks serious enough to me,' Madge gulped. 'Oh, Sam, what am I to do?'

'Bandage me up!' he snapped. 'Let's not get too self-pitying over this. It's all been said till we're both sick of it, Madge. As you make your bed, so shall you lie!'

'Don't be heartless, Sam!'

'My trouble is, Madge, I've got too much heart. Where you're concerned.'

'Did you think I was crying for myself?' she asked brokenly.

His mood changed slightly, and he grinned in a moment of wry tenderness. 'If a few of those tears were for me, don't waste any more. I'm still in the land of the living, my dear, and, by God, that's where I intend to stay!'

Madge squared her shoulders and swallowed hard, looking altogether more resolute. 'I'll tear up a sheet and make some bandages.'

'You do that,' he agreed.

She left the kitchen. Creed heard her walk through to her bedroom – where he presumed the sheet-tearing was to take place – and he pulled off his shirt in a single quick movement, suffering the pains of his rash action without a blink, and then went to the sink and put the dipper into the bucket of water standing beside it. Lifting the rounded scoop, he set it on its flat bottom in the sink, and after that, reaching down a towel off a nearby rail, he soaked the drying material in the water and began bathing his hurt with all the care that he could muster – since it was in his own best interests that no vestige of dirt should be covered up during the bandaging to come – and, though he realised that hot water should have been used for the laving, he was satisfied by the job that he had done on himself when Madge reappeared with several lengths of white material hanging from her left hand and a pair of scissors in her right.

'Sit down, Sam,' Madge ordered, pulling out a chair from beneath the kitchen table.

Creed seated himself, lifting his arms above his head so that the woman could work on the wounded part of his torso.

'What did those polecats do with my horse?' he inquired.

'It's tied to the hitching post outside,' the woman replied. 'Hubert said he was going to sell it.'

'That's another profit he won't pocket,' Creed hissed, shaking his head as she spoke the word 'salve' and turned away from him, her gaze moving around the room in a searching fashion. 'Don't bother with ointments and remedies, Madge. Plain clean and dry is best. I've got healing flesh.'

'If that's how you want it,' she said, and began the bandaging.

Creed watched her work with some fascination. Her fingers were nimble and swift, and she had a wonderful eye for measuring and tearing. Within five minutes, she had done an excellent job of binding him up and he was able to stand up again and flex himself, if gingerly. 'Thanks,' he said, jerking his head in satisfaction and then picking up his torn and bloody shirt and pulling it on again.

'You can't go out looking like that,' Madge said. 'Let me get you one of Hubert's shirts to put on.'

'Not likely!' Creed returned savagely. 'I'd rather go naked first!'

'Sam, hatred is a wicked thing.'

'I'm not trying to become a saint,' Creed retorted. 'I've seen what wickedness really is. Bad men never reform. Revenge is rough justice. The punishment must fit the crime. An eye for an eye, a tooth for a tooth. Put it how you like. You have to fight fire with fire. The rest is worthless cant – spouted by Bible-thumpers who have never encountered real wickedness in their lives.'

'You're growing into a mighty hard man, Sam.'

'I've got to be,' Creed said glumly. 'What are we to do about you, Madge? Why don't you take that face of yours back to Cheyenne for your ma and pa to see?'

'What do you imagine that would achieve?'

'If you were my daughter, Madge, I'd tell you to stay at home and let your husband go to hell.'

'My dad would have no sympathy,' Madge said desolately, 'and mama would go along with whatever he said.'

'I've a good mind to point my finger at that father of yours,' Creed rasped. 'I'll swear he's to blame for all your misery.'

'Whatever hurts him, Sam, must hurt my mother and me,' Madge gestured resignedly. 'I'm glad you're still alive, and I've the feeling that whatever you do next will do Hubert and his friends no good. It's all got to sort itself out, boy. I'm going to stay up here and see what comes out of that.'

'As good a place as any, I suppose,' Creed said blankly. 'You could go down to your in-laws in Ganville but they'll be on Hubert's side whatever happens. Sure, stay in the cabin. You're the mistress up here. Go to bed. Have a sleep. Forget.'

'Not a bad idea,' she sighed. 'Are you going to – Cutman's Pass?'

'Unless I badly miss my guess, that's where your husband has gone.'

'I heard him and his boys mention the place.'

'Do you know what those guys took there?'

She shook her head.

'Dynamite.'

'Is that what was in the–?' She broke off, aghast.

'In the locked shed, yes,' he completed for her. 'Your Hubie is some pet to have around the house, Madge!'

'What a pity that stuff didn't send him, me, and everything else up to heaven!'

'I reckon it must be easy for you to feel like

that right now,' Creed commented. 'You'll see things in another light tomorrow.' He looked towards the way out in the eastern wall of the kitchen. 'Guess I'm off.'

'A moment, Sam.'

'What?'

'When shall I see you again?'

'Put it like this,' he responded judiciously. 'If you see your husband again, it's unlikely you'll ever be seeing me again. But if you see me at your door – it's likely you'll be getting bad news of Hubert. Let's leave it there, eh?'

'You're a man without a gun,' she observed.

'Lost it when I took my tumble,' he answered, knowing that he must have dropped his sixgun during his fall between that high place and the torrent. 'Have you got one in here I can beg of you?'

'No.'

He figured that she had just told him a direct lie. Yet, perhaps perversely, he was glad of it. For it would have troubled him to take a gun from her hands with which he might yet end her husband's life. Nor would it have helped Madge's state of mind a lot. This way or that, she already seemed to be carrying a large enough burden of guilt. 'So long,' he said.

Two seconds later he was outside again. He saw his horse standing at the kitchen hitching post where Madge had said it was tied. Freeing the beast, he turned its head northwards and stepped up. After that he spurred for the end of the dwelling, rounded it and then headed westwards, re-entering the forest and following the path beyond the cabin back through the fir trees and on down to the ford, where he crossed over and picked up the continuation of the trail into the unfamiliar scene that he now judged to lie between him and the line of the railroad.

His mind was again active, but once more his motives in all this troubled and confused him. Nothing in this business – which was simple enough in essence – had ever appeared straightforward or actually remained so. He didn't really want to be involved, had no official right to be involved, and yet didn't want to skip his involvement. His revenge motives were too strong for that – on account of Wilf Mansell, Madge, and his own persisting sense of duty to the Union Pacific – and there seemed to be a welter of smaller things too that added up to an atmosphere of outrage which must be resolved before he could feel any peace of mind. At least, he no longer felt any deep hurt or corroding bitterness over the fact of Madge's marriage, and that was a bonus of the best sort. He was convinced now that all concerning the matter should be put down to circumstance, for it had little to do with him or her that was real, and that the woman had simply acted in what she had regarded as the best interests of her family. He would not have behaved as she had done himself – but then, Madge's family was not his family, and different loyalties were often expected from a daughter than a son. Whatever the final outcome of these doings, he would still be able to think of Madge with friendship and fondness, and he knew that he could expect nothing more. Nor would he let himself toy with any possibility beyond it.

The afternoon was very hot and still, and Creed's sodden garments had long since fully dried on him. His wound smarted under its dressing, and the muscles of his upper body were uncommonly stiff. He stirred up his horse, and the brute trotted that much faster for fifty yards or more, but soon fell back into its earlier plodding lethargy. The woodland sweated in Creed's nostrils, and the green distance rolled low and flat, a suspicion of cloud hanging in the mountain passes and dimming the sun-shot heavens where the greater Rockies thrust up their jagged shadows along the western skyline.

Soon the trail turned to parallel the railroad. Creed turned with it, dropping a little south of west. A kingfisher flew in from a lake that shimmered brightly through hanging foliage on the horseman's right, hovered for an instant above his pommel – as if it would settle – then banked away, a rainbow flash in the lazy glow of the sap-filled hour. Familiar with the entire length of the ironroad, from Des Moines to Sacramento, Creed soon realised that he was nearing Cutman's Pass, and he began to ride even more watchfully than was his habit – since Cutman's was more than three miles long and he did not wish to blunder upon Eichmann and party at some spot where he did not expect to find them – for he accepted readily enough that his own selection of the right place to set a charge of dynamite need not be the young gang boss's also.

Yet, despite his care in the matter, Creed almost did what he was trying to avoid. Tending to forget that a tightly snaking trail could bring a man all too suddenly up to the unexpected, he was in the process of rounding the end of a wall of stone which had suddenly outcropped on his left, when he almost rode full butt into Hubert Eichmann and friends. The young crooks, reins in hands and grey boxes at their feet, were standing in the circle of their horses and arguing loudly among themselves. It was the very noise that they were making, and the intensity of their concentration upon it, that allowed Creed to halt, dismount, and softly back up his horse into a position behind the corner where it could no longer be seen.

That done, Creed advanced again. Using the angle of the rock to conceal his presence, he eased his nose forward and peeped around the corner, seeing that Eichmann and company had already ground-tied their mounts on a piece of open ground to the right of the trail, picked up their boxes, and were now filing after their leader up the fairly steep and boulder-strewn slope to their left. With burdens on their shoulders, they were making for the ridge not far above them and overlooking the railroad tracks.

At a guess, this must be the place where the crooks were going to set their dynamite, ready for the hold-up tomorrow night. Then something clicked inside Creed's head. Was that it? He recalled that moment not so long ago when his sudden inspiration had fled, leaving that question mark branded on his mind. Was it possible that everything was now going to happen twenty-four hours early? And why not? The law knew about the robbery scheduled at Cutman's Pass for the night of July eighth, and Morgan Target would have spoken to George Binns about the matter. Binns, as the manager of the Cheyenne depot, had some power up and down the Union Pacific line and, assuming he had passed word of the forthcoming robbery to head office in Des Moines – with the recommendation that Sacramento ship their gold a day early – it was entirely possible that tonight's Flyer would be carrying the bullion from California.

At this stage, of course, it was just something that might be. Creed could be certain of nothing. But if he could get close to the crooks and eavesdrop their talk, he might in due course hear words that would confirm his suspicions. The thing must be taken as far as it would go.

With that conviction in mind, Creed started moving after Eichmann and party with stealth and determination.

EIGHT

Hurrying forward in a deep crouch, Creed reached the bottom of the slope up which the loaded men ahead of him were still toiling. He paused there in the cover of a large boulder. Then, about half a minute later, after seeing the climbers reach the top of their ascent and pass over the ridge itself, disappearing down the other side, he resumed his pursuit at a rapid scramble, arriving at the summit of the acclivity in about a third of the time that it had taken the burdened outlaws.

Dropping behind the rimrock itself, Creed peered over and below, expecting to see Eichmann and his friends walking down a similar slope to that up which he had himself just climbed. Instead – though the slope he had imagined did exist as an extensive presence beneath him – he saw Eichmann and company standing on a mass of granite that jutted out from the main angle of the descent and formed a considerable overhang above the ground about a hundred feet below on which the railroad track had been built in a long curve that reached back into the ground shadows of the west and a glimpse of the great trestle bridge which crossed the North Platte river.

Creed studied the men and their position below him with a concentrated stare. But it was another of those occasions when a watcher didn't need superior intelligence to work out what others had in mind. Yes, bring down that mass of overhanging rock on the track below and the railroad would indeed be blocked to the Flyer. But it would also be sealed to all trains from either direction. And that was very important too. For the rubble created would require days of hard labour to clear, while the way itself would have to be regraded and the rails laid anew. In fact, as Creed worked it out by rule of thumb, the Union Pacific's transcontinental service would be at a standstill for a week or more, and that would be a worse blow to the country – let alone U.P – than the theft of the Californian gold itself. Once again he hardened his determination to stop this projected crime with its possibly far-reaching consequences from taking place.

But the will to do was only a powerful

force when everything else supported it, and very little bolstered it here. The men below, though talking quite freely among themselves again, were way out of earshot. No words of theirs, innocent or guilty, reached him up here. In order to get even fairly close to them, he would need to creep down across a slope that had little or no cover on it in the vicinity of the overhang. If he attempted such a manoeuvre, he would certainly be seen before he got anywhere near the men below and probably killed on the spot. Worst of all, his death would amount to a form of suicide, and that would help nobody. There really was nothing for it but to hang on up here in the hope that events would soon contrive to bring about a change that would favour his purpose.

It was almost as if his need amounted to an unspoken prayer, for what amounted to an answer came pretty well at once. Suddenly, all save two men among those standing on the overhang turned to the right and stepped off the jutting vantage, leaving all the grey boxes behind them; and, as they walked down towards the ironroad, the pair who remained higher up began breaking out loose stone from the surface rock at the back of the natural platform and obviously preparing a slightly sunken bed in which the boxes of dynamite could lie and produce the kind of explosion which would break the overhang away from the slope to which it belonged.

The task was fairly arduous, and ought not to have been tackled without tools. Thus, the two men employed on the removal work had to give it all their energy and attention. This meant that, with the other four crooks now walking the track below and having no clear view of the slope above them, Creed was able to cross the ridge before him and crab downwards through whatever cover was available, coming soon to a spot where a boulder canted within a few yards of the two labourers who were still plucking rotten stone out of the hole that they were trying to make.

Sinking down to kneel uncomfortably behind the rock, Creed strained his ears at the pair on whom he was spying but, as he might have anticipated, they had little to say to each other as they levered out slabs of layered rock with their bare hands or pistol barrels and cast them aside. So, even though he was within the earshot that he had sought, his uneasy proximity to the two workers was of no more real value to him than watching them from the ridge above had been.

Time went by. The two men nearby cursed a good deal – over small cuts and broken fingernails for the most part – but still no word passed between them that was the least bit helpful, and the watcher had soon to admit to himself that his actions here had so far been misjudged. He felt this even more acutely when the pair opposite straightened up by tacit agreement, apparently satisfied with their crude excavation work, and got the 'makings' out, plainly intent on taking a rest. The peeping Creed watched them roll and light cigarettes – which seemed sheer madness to him in the presence of those grey boxes – but, despite flaming matches being thrown aside, no harm resulted and it began to seem to the watcher that the rest of the afternoon would wear itself away with nothing more achieved. Still more to the point, Creed began to fear that his presence behind the boulder would be eventually detected when the four men below finally climbed back up here and started saunter-ing around on the upper slope in much the same manner as they were now idling about on either side of the ironroad beneath.

The frustration became almost unbearable. Creed felt the tension crawling through his scalp and brainstem. He endured, sure that delivery would come – but, when it did, the form it took was totally unexpected; for the taller of the two young men on the overhang snapped back his head abruptly and shot out an arm, shouting as he pointed into the land off to the south of the railroad tracks, where a horseman had just emerged from the bushes at the forest edge and was now heading for the present spot.

Rousing from his recent nervous suffering with a jolt, Creed almost raised his head too high in fixing his gaze on the still fairly distant newcomer, but he managed to avoid giving his presence away to the pair of crooks nearby and sank down as low as he could while concentrating more and more intently on the big, lolloping rider coming in from the south. Already convinced that he knew the man – who, from his lack of posture, filled a saddle very seldomly indeed – Creed let himself feel nothing definite until the other was completely in focus, and then he allowed a wave of exultation to surge through him, for he found himself justified in both his recent deductions and instinctive feelings. The horseman was unquestionably George Binns, and the arrival of the Cheyenne railroad depot's manager here was proof that he was behind the threat to the gold from Sacramento and that the bullion shipment's date had been brought forward by twenty-four hours. Again everything fitted exactly, for, despite his position of authority, Binns would not be able to avoid suspicion falling upon him instantly if the stopping of the Flyer did now occur, and it was clear that the manager had ridden here from Cheyenne with the intention of fleeing his railroad job and being on the spot to pick up his share of the Sacramento gold which, it had to be assumed, would be big enough to put him on easy street for the rest of his life.

How to handle the situation for the best was once more Creed's crying need. There was too much to this business to attempt thwarting the hold-up all by himself. If the halting of the Flyer had been planned for daylight, he might have been able to prevent the robbery on his own; but, with it all down to happen after dark – even allowing for the presence of a good moon – it would be too much to expect of himself. He had sound eyes, and his share of ingenuity, but he was opposed by some desperate enemies – made the more formidable now that Binns had joined them – and he was also sufficiently hurt to be below his best. There were limits. He must have some help with this. Help from Morgan Target – if possible.

The telegraph was Creed's first aid, and the ironroad his second. If he could get a telegram to Target, explaining his need, the railroad should be able to put a locomotive on at Cheyenne and run out here with a horse car and posse. If all went smoothly, or anything like, two hours ought to see one of the new 2-4-2's puffing into the district. Given that Target and the posse could manage to leave Cheyenne by mid-evening, there ought to be enough time for them to get here and help put a stop to what the Binns/Eichmann gang was up to. Yes, it was all a matter of getting to a key. The nearest telegraph shack was at Flegg's Halt, about five miles to the west of Cutman's Pass. If he could contrive to withdraw from this slope unseen, there was no reason why he shouldn't have his message to Target on the wires in less than an hour.

Just then Creed heard the sound of feet running down the slope below the over-hang. He shifted his position a little so that he could peer after the noises. He saw that the smaller of the two men who had been getting ready to set the dynamite had just left his companion and was skipping and dancing a rapid course downhill, dust flying up from his heels and small pieces of rock spraying away from his toes. 'What the heck!' yelled the bigger man aggrievedly. 'Where the blue blazes are you off to, Danson?'

'Want to see George!' Danson threw back across his shoulder. 'Want to have a yarn, Grummitt! He's always got some good stories about girls!'

'You shouldn't be hearin' stuff like that at your age!' Grummitt disapproved. 'George Binns is a dirty old varmint!'

'Yeah, yeah!' Danson mocked breathlessly, his barely controlled feet having already carried him past what might be regarded as the point of no return.

'We been given a job, boy!'

'Plenty o' time for that, Jimmy!' Danson insisted, his voice diminishing as it was influenced by the joint effects of increasing distance and breathlessness.

And that was it. Danson joined the men below and Grummitt remained standing on the overhang, right foot jamming up and down in time to his curses.

Creed felt the compulsion to act promptly. He judged that Grummitt would continue looking downwards for the next minute or two, perhaps sullenly repeating his imprecations, and he gambled on it – lifting into a crouch and starting to back off up the slope to his rear – but he had covered no more than a yard or so, when Grummitt seemed to detect his presence and quickly craned round, their eyes meeting in mutal startlement. 'Hot damn!' the outlaw gulped, as if at the sight of a ghost. 'It's you!'

This was no time for words. Creed gathered himself. The other man had a revolver. It was lying on the ground beside him – dusty from its abuse as a prising tool – and now Grummitt dipped at the knees and made a grab for it. At this Creed acted. He took three running steps down the face of the incline, then launched himself at the badman, his dive almost horizontal, and he caught Grummitt round the waist and bore him to the earth, the gun falling back to where it had lain before.

It was a considerable impact. Grummitt absorbed most of it, but he was a young man at the height of his strength and it needed far more than a heavy fall to put him out of action. He threw Creed off him, then jacked himself erect, fists clenching. Creed rose too, but only into a crouch – for his wound had begun stiffening while he was in hiding and he was starting to feel his day's loss of blood – so he had to think in terms of outsmarting Grummitt rather than beating him in a straight battering match with their fists.

In this kind of battle there were no rules, and mercy had no place. The contestants were simply required to do the maximum amount of damage to each other with the least effort. Creed knew that the top of his head was as hard as most crowns, and he propelled himself upwards – using the length of his frame like a missile – and the middle of his skull made full contact with the underside of Grummitt's chin. The outlaw went reeling and staggering away from the contact of bone on bone and, reaching the front of the overhang, tottered there an instant before falling into space and plunging from his opponent's sight.

Rubbing his scalp, Creed stood gasping from his effort, reckoning that the fall Grummitt had just taken must have killed the man; but he had no time to move forward and look over the front of the overhang to see. Still letting his drive to action take him as it would, he faced about and raced up the slope towards the ridge – hardly giving a thought as to how what had just happened would affect his earlier planning – and he was over the crest of the land and out of sight again before he heard any kind of reaction in his wake.

And this, so far as he could tell – as he sped down the reverse side of the ridge – amounted to no more than confused shouting, and he received the impression that all the men in the vicinity of the railroad tracks had been concentrating so hard on the last part of George Binns' approach that they had missed Grummitt's fall completely and had no clear idea of how he had come to tumble off the overhang and crash down on their level. If that were indeed the case, it was entirely probable that the outlaws would remain in ignorance of the fact that their comrade had fallen as the result of a fight on the ground higher up and develop no suspicion that he had fought with an assailant. It was also unlikely, when account was taken of the steep recession of the land between the rails and the ridge, that any member of the gang could have spotted Creed's flight up the slope above the overhang, so it was quite possible that he was already clear of the scene and away and that no inkling of his presence would emerge at all. To him, in full knowledge of what had actually occurred, that seemed almost incredible, but happenings in life were often like that and, feeling an instinctive confidence in his summing up of probabilities, he decided to act as if his reasoning was a certainty all through and carry on from there as he had previously intended. If he made a mistake, there were sure to be signs of pursuit to tell him, and he could then vary his programme to get the best he could out of whatever form the flight forced on him took. As ever, he could do no more than circumstances permitted.

Coming again to the place where his horse stood, Creed swung up into his saddle. Then, riding past the bottom of the acclivity down which he had come running a minute ago, middled the trail and kept galloping in line with the railroad. His pace soon carried him out of the area occupied by the crooks and, within fifteen minutes, he was three miles on and not one of his several glances back had revealed anything on the trail behind him to worry about. All the same, when about a mile short of Flegg's Halt, ever cautious, he pulled off the trail and round to the rear of a clump of evergreens – holding motionless as he waited to see whether riders did come along – but the beaten way to the east of him remained as empty as ever and he rode back onto the track again, feeling certain now that all was indeed well. After that he spurred for the Halt and arrived there in the stilly, clinging heat of the late afternoon.

Flegg's amounted to a single wooden storage shed and the telegraph office. To the right of it, standing amidst the thinned out oaks and elms well short of a line of crumbling bluffs, were a few cabins and a saloon, remnants from the days when the railroad had been under construction, but Creed had no interest in their presence just then. Dismounting as near to the door of the telegraph shack as he could get, he went straight inside and banged a fist on the operator's desk, demanding instant attention from one who knew him a little from his years of sleuthing up and down the ironroad. 'Hi, Tyler,' he greeted, lifting a finger to his temple in salute as he grinned tightly at the round-shouldered incumbent of the Morse key. 'This is urgent – and then plenty. It's a message for County Sheriff

Morgan Target of Cheyenne. Are you ready?'

'Get on with it, Mr Creed,' the short-sighted telegrapher urged, peering up owlishly through the lenses of his steel-rimmed glasses, for he had instantly set aside other things to pick up his message pad and pencil.

'Cutman's Pass job brought up twenty-four hours,' Creed dictated. 'Gang already present. Vitally urgent you be here by dark. Bring posse. Signed Sam Creed.'

'Sounds like you've been busy,' Walt Tyler reflected, pulling a face as he read over what he had written down. 'Can't say I like the look of this.'

'Just get it on the wire to Cheyenne,' Creed ordered, 'and all should be well.'

'You hope,' Tyler sniffed, rattling out the Cheyenne call sign and adding a letter which denoted that the telegram coming through carried the highest priority. He received a blur of dots and dashes in return, and said that these told him the line was clear and his colleague in the Cheyenne office was waiting. Then Tyler rattled Creed's message off, the work of twenty seconds, and within moments after that got his receipt from the other end. 'Okay, Mr

Creed. Morgan Target should be reading your words quite soon now.'

'Good,' Creed acknowledged. 'What time should the Flyer hit Cutman's Pass tonight?'

'Half eleven.'

'The engineer's going at top speed through there, isn't he?'

'Believe so.'

'Will the Flyer have stopped at Fort Bridge yet?'

Tyler glanced up at the round-faced clock above his banks of accumulators. 'Before long.'

'You'd better get on that key again,' Creed said. 'We should advise caution through Cutman's Pass tonight. A pile-up is the last thing we want to risk. There is dynamite involved.'

'On the train?'

'Hell, no! The usual thing.'

'So what is on that train tonight?'

'If you don't know,' Creed returned, 'I can't tell you, Tyler.'

'Five dollars, forty red cents, and Abe Lincoln's wisdom tooth?' suggested a drawling male voice from the doorway.

Creed turned swiftly. Those mocking tones had been very familiar to him a few years ago. Yes, it was indeed Billy Norton standing on the threshold. Billy had been a good friend and the best of the railroad detectives. An independent and rather unpredictable character, he never should have resigned from his job with the Union Pacific, but boredom had got to him, or so he'd said. 'Well met, Billy!' Creed greeted heartily, thrusting out a hand.

Norton advanced, big and square, and his fearless gaze was level with Creed's own. Their hands met and clasped, then pumped briefly up and down. 'What have you been doing, Samuel?'

'Got creased,' Creed replied, touching the left side of his torn and stained shirt. 'A big shindig earlier in the day. A little one anyhow.'

'If you will play with guns.'

'It's not the guns. You can't blame the guns.'

'That old chestnut.'

'No, pal – Hubert Eichmann.'

'I heard they'd paroled that skunk,' Norton commented. 'Married Madge Stacey last week, didn't he?'

Creed scowled, then asked waspishly: 'Is there anybody in the territory who hasn't heard about that?'

'Sensitive!' Norton tut-tutted. 'More fish

in the sea, boy.'

'What changes?' Creed wondered sardonically. 'You always did enjoy taking the juice out of me, Billy. If you'd been anybody else, I'd have given you a cut of the skull long ago.'

'Sam!' Norton laughed. 'I'd be sure to hit you back.'

'Maybe even harder,' Creed admitted wryly. 'Perhaps that's why I haven't given you one.'

'What's a bloody nose between friends?'

'Not a damned thing!' Creed conceded, shrugging. 'What are you doing these days?'

'Not a damned thing!' Norton echoed, grinning.

'Gentleman of leisure, eh?'

'Gentleman, yes – but where's the leisure?'

'Broke?'

'Flat.'

'Wine, women and song.'

'Women, wine and song,' Norton laughed. 'You never could get that one right.'

'I'm a cough drop,' Creed allowed, smile slipping a trifle, for he had just had an idea. It wasn't a very good one, but he was desperate, and Billy Norton had been known to do crazy and reckless things when broke – and suddenly prompted into them.

162

'Want a job, Billy?'

'I've been long enough out of my last one,' Norton confessed. 'I was riding shotgun on the Green river. Gun job?'

'Would I be likely to offer you anything else?'

'Guess not. To do with tonight's Flyer?'

'How much did you overhear?'

'All of it, I think.'

'Yes, to do with the Flyer. Even if I wouldn't tell Walt Tyler, I'll have to tell you. There's a big shipment of gold from Sacramento that will pass through these parts tonight.'

'Regular thing, isn't it?' Norton said dismissively. 'Are you asking on your own behalf or the Union Pacific's?'

'No, pal. Acting on behalf of myself. I'm no longer on the company's active list. This is one I'm doing mainly for myself.' Creed tapped the money-belt that he was still wearing. 'You'll be working for me, and I'll be paying you.'

'How much?'

'A hundred dollars.'

'How long?'

'Say, breakfast tomorrow.'

Pulling an appreciative jib, Norton scratched delicately at the tip of his nose.

'Good rate of pay, Sam. Would cover a first class funeral.'

'I'm not going to ask you to commit suicide, noodle!' Creed snorted. 'Did you ever know me to take a risk I didn't have to take?'

'Often.'

'Thank you,' Creed said sourly. 'Well, for want of better words, I hope we'll be doing no more than keep a watchful eye on what's presently happening in Cutman's Pass. Eichmann and company – plus George Binns from Cheyenne – are planning to blast an overhang down onto the tracks. If you heard everything just now, you'll be aware that I've sent for Morgan Target and a posse. It's just that I don't know – how it's all going to come out.'

'Well, that's a mighty fine admission!' Norton scoffed. 'What do we ever know for sure? It's life, Sam!' He chuckled mirthlessly to himself. 'A hundred dollars. That's a lot of money from a guy who never did chuck the stuff away. And Sam Creed's renowned for wanting his pound of flesh. Suicide? Just maybe. It's real dangerous on the feel of that evidence. Two hundred?'

Creed breathed in deeply and held the air. 'All right.'

'Um.'

'Where the devil else do you think you're going to get two hundred dollars for maybe fifteen hours' work? That kind of pay is worth some risk, isn't it?'

'I keep hearing that church bell, Sam.'

'Will you take the job, Billy?'

'For you.'

'You won't regret it.'

Norton turned back his head and laughed uproariously. 'No, but you may do, Sam!'

'That's a chance I'll have to take,' Creed observed, frowning to himself; for he could not help wondering why Billy Norton should have said such a thing.

NINE

There was silence between Creed and Norton as they left the telegraph office. Outside their horses were standing shoulder to shoulder in the shadow of the building, and the two men mounted up with practised ease. Creed indicated the trail that led eastwards, and they set their mounts trotting down it. Now Norton started asking questions about what was happening in Cutman's Pass. Answering the other openly where he could – but guardedly elsewhere – Creed provided much of his story since his arrival in Cheyenne yesterday afternoon. Within ten minutes of their leaving Flegg's Halt, Norton knew a large part of what there was to know concerning his employer's current affairs.

'Mind if I ask a question now, Billy?' Creed asked, when they were quiet again and had more or less halved their ride to Cutman's Pass. 'Where did you spring from?'

'When, Sam?'

'You know when,' Creed responded with a new hint of asperity. 'Just now – back there, in Walt Tyler's telegraph office.'

'Sort of coincidence, I guess,' Norton remarked carelessly. 'I've been riding this way from Rock Springs the last day or two. Happened to pause at Flegg's watering place.'

'So you've been drinking?'

'Too hot to drink anything but light beer,' Norton yawned. 'They give that to babies.'

'Alcohol's bad stuff.'

'You've had your share, Sam.'

'From time to time,' Creed admitted – 'and often wished I hadn't afterwards.'

'We're a long time dead.'

'That's another of those old chestnuts,' Creed said irritably. 'You're full of them.'

'Well, there,' Norton said indifferently. 'Do you know what made me reluctant back there?'

'Greed?'

'No. Your holster's empty.'

'I lost my gun in that torrent I told you about.'

'Is that why you hired mine?'

'It must have its place,' Creed confessed. 'Have you got a spare six-shooter in your gear?'

'I have.'

'You'd better let me have it then.'

'When you need it – boss.'

That riled Creed properly, and he felt inclined to insist upon the transfer – as a demonstration of his employer's right – but Norton's spare gun was, after all, Norton's own property, and he had no claim of any kind upon the weapon. In effect, he had simply asked a favour of his companion and Norton had the moral right to give or withhold – at his will and no other's – so Creed felt constrained to bite his tongue and say no more, though here again he had received a kind of response from Billy Norton that he would never have expected on his previous knowledge of the man.

He looked around him, giving his annoyance the chance to dissipate. They were riding through a piece of forest where the tree trunks were well-packed with undergrowth at ground level. Everything remained hot and still as the afternoon headed for evening, and this brought Creed an even greater sense of disquiet when he heard bursting noises from the bushes on his right and a horseman came charging into view, revolver in hand and obviously requiring a lot more than the time of day.

Indeed, the newcomer was now recognisable to Creed as Stanley Barstow, and Barstow yanked his mount's head round and stopped in the middle of the trail, his six-shooter pointing at Creed's chest. 'Halt!' he commanded.

'Get him, Billy!' Creed hissed, well aware of how fast his companion could draw and shoot.

The sunken-cheeked, evil-eyed Barstow grinned as Satan might have grinned at a netting of souls, the bullet-wound which his face had received that morning an inflamed and scarlet line upon his jaw. 'His gun's out, Creed!' he grated mockingly.

Mystified, Creed started turning his face towards Norton, but checked the movement instantly when steel pressed against the side of his head and he heard the metallic echoes of a hammer being cocked pass through the bone of his skull and into his brain. 'I see, Billy,' he said levelly. 'You've finally gone to the bad.'

'Depends on what you mean by that,' Norton said in the same even manner. 'It's not that I've actually turned into a crook, Sam, but I have finally wised up to how she spins. I've been shot at and taken every kind of abuse for small pay – mostly in the name of plain honesty – but now I've put myself up to be cursed and shot at in the name of the big money and a good life.' He jiggled the hammer of his Colt. 'Make sense?'

'Not to me,' Creed said. 'The good life's an illusion, and at best it's mighty short.' He paused to let his words sink in. 'Do you understand me?'

'Oh, it's Sam who knows everything,' Norton said agreeably enough. 'Sure, good and bad, you pursue a thing long enough and your luck runs out. I've seen it too – and remarked it in the head office at Des Moines. This is my one and only crooked job, Samuel. When it's done, it's me for the bright lights and the girls who are pretty.'

'Says you, Norton!' Barstow snarled. 'Tell it to George Binns. He may have other ideas.'

'Don't push your luck, Barstow!' Norton warned. 'Binns and I think the same way. Do it once, make it big, and go. That's where we're so different from Hubert Eichmann and his numskulls.'

'Think what you like,' Barstow returned disdainfully. 'I've run plenty of errands for George Binns. A corkscrew is a sight straighter than that man. Nor are you so clean, Norton. You had the odd taster from those wrecks a year or two back. George saw to it.'

'He knows why too,' Norton growled.

'What's it all coming out, Billy?' Creed asked through his teeth. 'Old friends or not, if you had anything to do with those smash-ups I'll see you hang!'

'I had nothing to do with the wrecks!' Norton protested, for he was clearly shaken by the power of Creed's threat. 'I found a cave filled with stuff that Binns and some of the staff had stolen off the wrecks.'

'You took hush money?'

'Favours, Sam – favours.'

'Like bonuses for jobs others had done?'

'Maybe.'

'Choices?'

'Perhaps.'

'Expenses you'd no right to?'

'What do you care, Sam?' Norton demanded angrily. 'I did no wrecking. The blood of the passengers who died in those crashes is on hands other than my own. Dammit! I left the Union Pacific, didn't I?'

'It makes no difference,' Creed said implacably. 'You benefited from what happened. I'd hang you on the same beam as the rest of them.'

'You're a bastard when you get your knife

in, Creed!' Norton declared.

'He'll shortly be a dead one, I reckon,' Barstow said. 'He knows too much. There's only one way for him.'

'Eichmann and knuckleheads have had one go at him today, according to what he told me,' Norton said. 'I'd kill him now, but I want Hubert Eichmann to see what an amateur he is without Norman Trevelyan.'

'Won't do them any harm to realise what could have happened if you and me hadn't been riding here late and spotted him sneaking away from Cutman's Pass,' Barstow said. 'I reckon we handled following him to Flegg's Halt pretty damn well. I'll swear he never suspected, despite how canny he is.'

'Trouble is,' Norton observed heavily, 'the harm's done, Barstow. He's called up Cheyenne. Morgan Target will be coming to Cutman's by train – with a posse.'

'That's a proper foul-up!' Barstow declared, swearing sulphurously. 'Sounds like we lose everything!'

'Doesn't have to be so,' Norton said uncertainly. 'Remember, we do know what's on board. Everything depends on how much we're prepared to do about it. That's to say, what we have in the way of guts.'

'Don't know for that, Billy,' Barstow growled. 'I'm no man for putting in more than the job's worth.'

'What if the job's worth a heap?' Norton inquired. 'You're the guy who carried the figures here.'

'From George Binns.'

'Then we'll have our say to George,' Norton said, 'and hear what he thinks.'

'That's jake with me,' Barstow acknowledged, abruptly decisive. 'Let's steer Creed into Cutman's Pass.'

'Righto,' Norton agreed. 'But let's not do it the hard way and go in over the top. All we have to do is turn off through the trees not far from here and pick up the railroad just short of where the Pass begins.'

'I'll go along with that too,' Barstow said, fetching his horse about. 'Come on.'

Giving the hammer of his Colt another little jiggle, Norton grinned knowingly at the captive Creed. 'Are you going to be sensible, Sam?'

Creed nodded emphatically. 'I sure am. Because I've got a new ambition, Billy. It's to see you hit the end of that rope!'

'Cruel man!' Norton taunted. 'Move your butt, son!'

Creed stirred his horse into motion. He

moved up behind Barstow, and Norton fell in behind him. They followed the trail eastwards for another three or four hundred yards; then, at a word from Norton, turned off to the right where a game track was visible. After that they rode through the trees and undergrowth – to some extent forcing their passage where the brush and hanging foliage were thick – but they had not yet travelled very far when they emerged from the woodland on the edge of a shallow cutting and were able to descend without difficulty to the railroad below. Here, not shy of the tracks themselves, they turned left and then rode on into the slowly deepening V of Cutman's Pass, green walls that were ribbed with grey stone climbing near them at first and then falling back on the right with the southward curve of the rails just here to bring into view the overhang and other details of the Cutman's scene with which Creed had become familiar during the time that he had spent hidden high up on the slope overlooking the place from the north.

It remained a matter of keeping the progress steady, and it wasn't long before Creed saw figures on the land up front. Shortly after that, those figures did some obvious return spotting, and the faces of George Binns, Hubert Eichmann, Danson, and the other men who were less familiar, screwed towards the riders coming along the Pass, and some consternation was apparent among the watchers as the identity of the prisoner with their two colleagues became apparent to them. The badmen, all on foot – and led by the bulky, rubicund George Binns – walked forward rather tentatively to join the newcomers and, when the meeting occurred – perhaps fifty yards west of the overhang's jutting presence – every man halted in silence. Then Hubert Eichmann, scared-looking at first and then blusteringly belligerent, stabbed out a finger at Creed and bawled: 'Where'd you dig that rattler up from, Barstow? He's dead as a doornail!'

'Hold your silly noise, Hubert!' Binns advised. 'He's no such thing, and well you can see it! You are a blundering nincompoop! That's Sam Creed, and it's known he won't die easily!'

'Much as he needs to, George!' Norton added; then went on to repeat the story of how, on making their earlier approach to Cutman's Pass, he and Barstow had spotted Creed leaving the place and then shadowed him to Flegg's Halt, where Norton had overheard the railroad detective's telegraph message to Cheyenne. The facts of the telegram, and what they actually meant, were a little slow to sink in among the outlaws; but, after they had, there was an outburst of cursing and swearing such as Creed had never heard equalled; and the sheer hatred with which all eyes fixed on him should have been enough to kill. 'He's been and gone and done it!' Hubert Eichmann raged, his face taking on a slavering bestiality as his little moustaches gathered up into his nostrils and his teeth showed. 'If Morg Target's coming, we'd best be going! Let's all put a bullet in Sam Creed!'

'Keep your head, boy,' Binns ordered – 'keep your head!'

'Dreadful, isn't it?' Norton commented, a bony, heavy muscled giant as he bent forward over his pommel and gazed down at Eichmann with every scrap of an adult's pained dislike for a naughty child. 'Norm Trevelyan must be spinning in his grave when he hears about you, Hubie!'

'Don't you call me Hubie!' Eichmann yapped. 'That's what my ma calls me. I'm a man, d'you hear? Hubert or Hube.'

'Lord help us!' Norton appealed. 'Did you

ever hear the like?'

Binns gestured for silence all round. Then he threw a handkerchief at Eichmann, who was almost blubbering by this time. 'What do you think about it, Billy?' he asked.

'The same as you, I imagine,' Norton answered. 'We have two choices. The first is ride away. The second is meet the train from Cheyenne this evening and ambush Target and his posse. The loco isn't going to stop too far away from here. The county sheriff won't work any harder than he must, and he'll be expecting to hand it out – not receive it.'

'My thought exactly,' Binns acknowledged. 'What's your view of it, Barstow?'

'Shaky,' the go-between replied. 'There's no hangman in it yet.'

'There's no anything in it as matters stand,' Binns remained soberly. 'We'll never have another chance like this. There's eight of us here, and we can all shoot. If we keep our nerve, we'll have that posse cold, and Target will never dream we're waiting. A couple of volleys should do it.' He reflected for a moment on what he had already said, then added: 'We're fairly remote out here, and the local law will be in a real tizzy with Morgan Target dead and gone. We should have ample time to get away after we've turned to and robbed the Flyer – even burdened with the gold.'

'If the worst comes to the worst,' Norton added, 'we know more hiding places around Wyoming than most. The gold will have to be put into one of them for the time being. We can leave the territory until the hue and cry has died down. I'd prefer no killing, but I don't see any other way now, boys, and there's always some risk and hardship. Nothing comes but what you put yourself out to get it. That includes gains of the ill-gotten sort.'

'Spoken like an honest man, Billy!' Binns jibed. 'But true enough for all that. Hear, Eichmann?'

'I hear you,' the young gang-boss replied sullenly. 'Eight of us, you say. That's no army. It should've been nine. I've got an idea it was Sam Creed who threw Jimmy Grummitt off that rock up there. I knew Jimmy. He wouldn't just have blundered off. No, sir! It was Sam Creed's doing.'

'What's this, George?' Norton asked. 'Have I missed something?'

'They've lost a man,' Binns explained, glancing round and up towards the over-hang. 'Seems he fell off that lump of jutting stone. The boy's neck was broken. I suppose it's possible Creed was responsible. Even likely. Given what you and Barstow saw to begin with.'

'Well, Sam?' Norton queried.

Creed had not told Norton the facts of Grummitt's demise before, and he was not going to now. He simply sat his horse and kept quiet.

'Shoot him!' Eichmann begged.

'Just your style, Hubie,' Creed goaded. 'All you're any good for is scaring girls and robbing piggy banks.'

'You get off that horse!' Eichmann raved. 'I'll give you what for!'

'Like you gave your wife?' Creed gritted. 'Sure, you bullying weasel, I'll take you on. Even if I have only the one sound arm!'

'Cut that out!' George Binns roared. 'Eichmann, he'd be too good for you if he had both hands tied behind his back and was lame of a leg! We don't want anybody else hurt. Is that dynamite set up and ready to blow?'

'Phil?' Eichmann inquired, just about managing to control himself in the face of Binns' anger.

'You know it ain't!' the fellow that Creed knew as Danson responded, looking sheepish. 'I ain't been back up there since poor Jimmy went and fell.'

'Then you'd better get up there pretty damned smart before long!' Eichmann warned. 'Time's wastin', and we don't want things driven up!'

'Those are the first true words I've heard you speak since I got here,' Binns said. 'Do you want to shoot Sam Creed?'

'Does a fish need water?' Eichmann demanded ferociously, pulling out his revolver.

'All right,' Binns said. 'You might as well get it over with. Step down, Sam.'

Creed made to obey, sucking air into his lungs for all he was worth. Then a train whistled behind the next bend to the east and not more than a quarter of a mile away. Heads turned sharply towards the noise, and Binns let out a cry of annoyance. 'I'd forgotten about that!' he announced. 'Me, of all people! It's the afternoon freight from Cheyenne!' He pointed along the side of the tracks. 'Hide that dead man! Get the horses clear of the rails! Try to make it look as if we're a railroad party camping out!'

The burst of activity that followed was spontaneous and considerable. Hurrying men fanned eastwards across a narrow front to do Binns' bidding. Still in his saddle, Creed watched Eichmann dashing away with the rest. He breathed a sigh of relief. He had believed himself dead, but now his brain was racing, and he thought he had a chance.

It went like this. Until the freight train had passed, the situation favoured him more than anybody. But he must try to leave his horse at exactly the right instant, then spring across the ironroad a split second ahead of the oncoming locomotive. For he had recalled that there was a gun lying up there on the overhang. Grummitt's gun. If he could run up there and seize the pistol, his options would open up at once – with one particularly dangerous possibility appealing to him more than the rest – but everything was in flux right now and a single word or action could still make the difference between the sudden death for which he had appeared to be fated and a success that seemed to border on the impossible the harder he looked at it.

'Sam!'

It was Billy Norton calling to him. Creed played deaf.

'Sam, damn your eyes!'

'What? You did call, Billy?'

'Don't you, Billy me!' Norton roared. 'Get off that cuss-blamed nag of yours!'

The locomotive had just turned the bend and was rattling and swaying onwards at a nice pace, its whistle hooting and white smoke belching from the battered lozenge of its black steel funnel.

'What for?'

'Get off!'

Creed perceived that Billy Norton had worked himself into a real paddy. It was step down at once or take a bullet through the ribs. So Creed cocked his right leg, heaved up his backside – paused for a long moment – then fetched his bent leg the whole way over, hung for another instant on his nearside stirrup and dropped to the grass, looking up at Norton in feigned perplexity.

The train went on rushing towards the ground which the two men and their horses occupied. As he backed up towards Norton's mount, Creed could see the dirt and rust on the locomotive's cowcatcher and the roped down farm implements on the first of the flat-topped cars behind the tender. The detail was extremely vivid, and there was a sense of crude inevitability about the train's ponderous onrush.

'Get back – right back!' Norton yelled.

The seconds were clicking through Creed's brain with a ratchet-like precision, for the moment was almost here; but now Norton's horse had come surging forward to nudge at his left shoulder and force him aside. Creed reacted in the only way he could, lashing back at the brute's right foreleg with the rowels on the heel of his left boot. The steel teeth of the spur flayed hide and rasped against the bone, and the injured horse shrilled its agony and reared close to the vertical, its hooves swinging across the top of its assailant's head with several feet of clearance.

Creed sprang to his left while the chance was there. He faced the ironroad. Then, almost certain that he had left it too late – for the front of the locomotive now loomed within a yard or two of him and he could smell the monster's steam and hot oil – he launched himself into a bound that carried him just inches clear of the speeding cowcatcher and brought him down in a sprawling heap on the graded level at the other side of the tracks.

He had survived; but, scrambling up, Creed didn't ask himself how or consider the tiny margins involved. He simply pointed himself at the slope before him and began clawing and heaving upwards, generating a low-centred run against the steep tip of the acclivity, while the freight train rumbled past in his wake, its cars acting as a shield against the guns of the outlaws whom he could faintly hear shouting through the noise made by the train.

There was no pain in Creed any more. He no longer knew what fatigue meant. His running had every scrap of his energy in it and seemed inspired. Dirt and fragments of stone scattered and flew from under his boots just as similar debris might have done from beneath the pads of a rapidly tucking coyote. He kept going without any kind of check, and was nearing the middle slope by the time the freight train cleared the ground below. Now bullets spanged and jumped around him, and twice he was narrowly missed by shots that he suspected had come from Billy Norton's gun, but he was already a fair way up the acclivity and the angle at which the marksmen were required to shoot made luck rather than skill the greater element in scoring a hit.

He continued unscathed. Then he reached the level at which the overhang jutted. Turning right, he made a dash across the slope, ending at the rear of the thrusting rock, where the boxes of dynamite still lay scattered as before and Grummitt's revolver was also clearly visible. Going to the weapon, he picked it up, seeing that it had a fouled and unserviceable look about it, but he knew that a Colt revolver could take a lot of mishandling and still function well enough when so required.

Now Creed lifted his head and looked down the slope beneath him. The younger men from below were surging up the angle space, firing as they came, but the exercise kept them unsteady and no bullet passed close enough to cause him disquiet. Creed fixed his gaze on Hubert Eichmann. The young gang-boss was leading the climbers. Pared down to the last ounce, Eichmann was a long-limbed, perfectly functioning cat of a man, and this impression was enhanced by the wild brightness of his eyes, the whiteness of his large clenched teeth, and the sheer confidence of his presence as he sensed an end in view. He fancied himself with a gun, that much was very apparent, and the slow lift of his right hand betrayed that he was calculating his first blast at the fugitive with the utmost care.

Pistol cocked and ready, Creed stood his ground. It was all going to happen for him here or not at all. He had debated the moral and emotional issues before; but this had to happen. There was a woman between them, yes – and a natural hatred too – but there was also duty in all its aspects; for Eichmann needed killing; and, as his enemy came into sure range and their pistols balanced each other, he aimed deliberately for Eichmann's heart, and fired as the outlaw fired. Eichmann's bullet sang past his left ear, but his own slug drilled a hole exactly where he had intended, and the dark man opposite fell in his tracks and lay motionless. It was over between them. Creed knew that he had sent his enemy that wreath of gunsmoke.

But Creed also knew that there was still plenty more to come from other directions. Eichmann's young followers dried out and jerked to a halt at the sight of their fallen leader. Then, approaching him a moment later as a company of four, they bent and carried out a swift examination. 'He's dead!' Phil Danson suddenly announced, looking up sharply and casting Creed a glance of pure hatred. 'You've gone and killed Hubert, mister!'

'There's four of us!' reminded a ferrety little wretch, with patches of incipient baldness in his lank brown hair and gaps already present in his yellow and neglected teeth. 'We can kill him!'

'We sure can!' Danson agreed, straightening up and firing a miss as he spoke.

Creed dodged to his left. Yes, at four to one they would probably get him – if they kept their nerve – but, nerve or otherwise, he had no intention of allowing them to fire any more shots. Dropping behind a boulder, he deliberately aimed and fired at one of the boxes of high explosive that lay close to the hole that Grummitt and Danson had opened earlier to receive the dynamite with which the overhang was to be blasted down onto the ironroad below.

There was a blinding flash, an almighty crash, and a shaking of the slope that jarred Creed all through. Fumes, brown and sulphurous, mushroomed upwards where the four young crooks had been. Rocking and spreading, the smoke grew and grew into a cloud which soon covered much of the immediate slope above the railroad, and Creed coughed and choked in its midst, believing that he had achieved this purpose and eliminated the rest of Eichmann's gang without bringing down the mass of rock that jutted before him. But then, as he was trying to shake the ringing out of his ears, the very thing that he had been praying wouldn't happen did; for the heavily shaken overhang suddenly broke away from the rest of the slope and fell to the ground beneath, the tearing crash of the initial rupture blending with the showering roar of hundreds of tons of granite and lighter material building up into a heap below that must already have blocked the rail tracks entirely. The racket persisted for a second or two, then ceased, and there was just the renewed silence, the slowly thinning smoke – and the ringing in Creed's ears.

Kneeling forward, with arms flung over the top of the boulder before him, Creed watched and waited for the men below – who were presumably still alive and probably more dangerous than ever – to come climbing up here and make some new attempt to kill him. Well, he had a good field of fire and was ready to make his enemies smart when they tried it.

TEN

At least five minutes went by, and what Creed had anticipated did not happen. All remained quiet down below, and he was tempted to think that a game of nerves had been instituted. But he did not really see how George Binns, Billy Norton, and Stanley Barstow could afford to put their time into that. With the dynamite exploded and the overhang brought down far too soon, their original plan to halt the Flyer was in ruins. It seemed they would do well to remember that they were still free men and ride far and fast while the chance was still there. But when had a sane man ever been able to accurately predict the reactions of those made mad by disappointment?

Then, just as Creed fully got his hearing back, a shout came echoing up to him from Billy Norton. 'You all right, Sam?'

Creed kept silent, his mind straining as he tried to visualise a way out of the still considerable mess that he was in.

'Oh, Sam!' Norton protested. 'I know

you're still alive and kicking. Don't go coy on me, pal.'

'You can see the way up here, Billy!' Creed shouted back.

'Sure. I'll bet good money you've got it covered too!'

'Easy to find out.'

'Do you have to be such an unforgiving man?'

'Yes, when what I run up against is unforgivable.'

'For the good of your soul, man!'

'It's your body you're worried about, Billy boy!'

'There's no turning you, is there?'

Creed spat into the dust next to his boulder.

'Sam!' It was George Binns who was shouting up to him now.

'What do you want, Binns?'

'Haven't we seen enough deaths for one day?' Binns demanded. 'Do others have to die before you're satisfied?'

'Not if you men give up and let me take you in!'

'That's rather the point, isn't it?' Binns queried, perhaps a trifle enigmatically.

'Like to make that plainer, Binns?'

'You've separated the men from the boys.'

'Something like that has happened,' Creed agreed.

'So why don't we behave like adults?'

'And do what?'

'We've been talking it over down here, Sam.'

'Now that does surprise me!'

'We're four good men.'

'One good one,' Creed corrected, 'and three bad ones.'

'Listen to that donkey braying again!' Norton's voice interrupted. 'Are you trying to bore us to death, Sam? Tales of virtue cut no ice here. Are you so dumb you can't see we're making you an offer? The job's clearly off here – for all sorts of reasons; including the most important one: that you've made the law aware of it.

'Okay? No hard feelings, Sam! We're past all that. We just want what's best for each and every one. Yes, we need you, boy! Four of us could manage a job that three might fail on. I'm talking about stopping the Flyer at Flegg's Halt. You've already put some worry into that run. The engineer will be coming through with his throttle half shut, and he'll be a mighty watchful man. I promise you he won't miss a guy swinging a red lamp on the line ahead of him. He'll stop that train, and the guy with the lamp will then spin him a good yarn to keep him there, while our other three go aboard – as good where seems best – and clear out the express car. It's done, Sam, before anybody at the front of the train has got more than half a notion of what's happened. And we're four rich men. Neat, eh?'

Creed opened his mouth, but found himself too amazed to answer.

'Well, what do you say, Sam?' Norton demanded. 'I reckon it's a better plan than the first one.'

'And stands even less chance of succeeding,' Creed assured him, frowning to himself in puzzlement. For there was something wrong with this. In the optimism of it all, which was surely spurious. The ever clear-witted Norton should know better than to try tempting him with a lame-brained scheme like this. There was a touch of tongue-in-cheek about it all. Binns and Norton were bunco-dealing. He was being deceived – and in the short term too. Those two were trying to divert his mind – for just long enough. There was something else going on here. What the deuce was it? His deeper mind sent him foraging. 'What does Stanley Barstow think about this, Billy?'

'He's leaving it to George and me,' Norton responded, just too airily.

That was it. Barstow. He was no longer with the two men below.

Sheerly on instinct, Creed threw himself to the left where the dirt on the ground was thickest, and in that same instant a shot rang out behind him and a bullet flattened against the side of the boulder that his torso had been covering throughout his verbal exchanges with the pair beneath.

Squirming round in the dirt, Creed brought up his six-shooter, judging where the gunshot had come from by ear and instantly spotting Barstow's erect presence before a reef of stone not a dozen yards away. Barstow had a rifle to his shoulder, and was pumping the ejector for a second try, but Creed got in first, and the shot he fired sent his would-be killer staggering. Once more Creed thumbed back his hammer, ready to let the other man fall if he would, but Barstow managed to hold his feet and fought to bring his Winchester into line for a hip shot. Creed triggered again and, though his bullet flew higher than he had intended, it got the job done nicely, for a third eye appeared in Barstow's forehead and he fell with all the rigidity of a dummy across the outcropping rock behind him. He lay still, and no further trace of movement showed in any part of him.

There was a pause while that last shot echoed into silence.

'Stanley!' Binns shouted suddenly.

'He's muffed it, you fool!' Creed heard Billy Norton snarl. 'That was a Colt!'

'Then we'll have to do it ourselves!' Binns declared, voice piping with fear. 'Come on!'

Creed listened hard, pistol at the ready. He heard stamping footfalls on the climb amidst slithering noises. This he could hardly credit. Binns had undoubtedly lost his nerve, and at least some of his panic must have affected Norton also. The crazy pair were charging uphill against a gun. This could prove too easy. If such a thing were possible.

Walking forward, Creed brought the climbing pair into full view. Sighting him, the onrushing duo promptly opened fire. Creed held his position among the flying slugs. Then he aimed at Binns, the larger target, and squeezed his trigger, scoring a solid hit. Screaming, the manager pitched forward onto his knees; then, reaching out, he grabbed the slack of Norton's trousers with his left hand and begged for help.

Checking, Norton tried to shake off Binns' grip, removing his eyes from the man above as he looked back and down. Seeing an advantage in this, Creed steadied his aim in such fashion as to feel certain that his next shot would knock the fight out of Norton once and for all; but his pistol had no sooner gone off than he heard his bullet collide with his erstwhile friend's advanced weapon and received the impression then of the slug jumping and rending muscle at the top of Norton's right shoulder. Though the wound thus caused was obviously a bad one, it was far from the crippling hurt that Creed had intended, when aiming at the other's stomach, and Norton attempted transferring his revolver to his left hand and carrying on the fight; but the encumbering presence of Binns in his wake finally compelled him to drop the gun and turn to the manager's assistance. 'Get up!' he raged. 'You got us into this – now help yourself!'

'Are you two ready to give up now?' Creed demanded.

'Go to the devil!' Norton flung back at him. 'You're holding an empty gun, Sam!'

Creed cocked and triggered. He discovered at once that Norton had counted his shots accurately – or at least pulled off a successful gamble – for his weapon clicked emptily and sent him diving to his belt for a reload. While he thumbed new bullets into his Colt, the two villains below him withdrew clumsily from the slope – with a vindictive Binns bawling at a reluctant Norton that 'everything concerning the past' would be revealed if the manager were taken by the law – a threat which obviously carried real terror for Norton, since he supported Binns as best he could until they reached two of the numerous horses now standing ownerless near the ironroad and then bumped him into the saddle. That done, he too mounted up and, slack in their seats and riding far from securely – for it was now clear that both had received severe wounds – they lit out south of west, heading for the tract of forest out of which Creed had seen Binns ride earlier on.

Thrusting his reloaded gun away, Creed now ran down the face of the slope himself. Reaching the bottom, he crossed the railroad tracks – which were less badly blocked to the left of him than he had expected them to be – and, unable to see his own mount, grabbed the first horse that he came to and spurred after the two riders ahead of him in the belief that he would overtake them before they reached the trees; but in fact the timber was closer than he had realised and Binns and Norton passed from view while he was still a few hundred yards behind them.

Creed was fairly relaxed as he entered the woodland. It might take a little while yet, but he anticipated few difficulties in overhauling the two fugitives and taking them prisoner. He was going to list their crimes, and then he was going to testify against them in court. After that they would either go to prison for a long, long time or he would step out one morning and see them hang. He felt justice would be done, and that was the right outcome for a business like this.

What in fact happened next was as big a surprise as any that he had received. For he was no distance into the trees at all, when Billy Norton – armed with a piece of a bough – sprang at him out of the shadows and let go at him obliquely with a left-handed blow. Struck across the chest, Creed left his saddle and landed heavily upon the ground behind his horse. Winded, but otherwise not greatly hurt, he rolled aside as Norton came at him, trying to bash his brains out. Gathering up his legs, he dodged this way and that, hoping that Norton – who was bleeding profusely from his shoulder wound – would soon exhaust himself; but the other appeared to recognise his purpose and attacked with greater and greater savagery. He hurt Creed anew with a pair of glancing blows to the upper body, reducing his mobility in the process, and the railroad detective jerked his gun and raised it threateningly. 'Cut it out, Billy!' he cautioned. 'I won't take much more!'

Norton redoubled his efforts to harm. The clubbing wood was everywhere again, and suddenly skidded across Creed's crown. His senses expanded redly, then shrank towards darkness, and he only just managed to retain his consciousness. He could risk no more; this had to stop immediately. Lifting his gun, he fired into his attacker's chest. Norton lurched backwards, knees bowing towards each other, and he looked down and grinned wanly as he saw the scarlet blood gushing from his latest wound. 'Thank you, Sam,' he said through a bubbling in his throat; and then he fell dead.

Creed glanced around him, rubbing at his abused scalp. Where had George Binns got to? He was fairly sure that there was nothing to fear from the manager, but he must not let himself become overconfident again. Moving cautiously, and with his eyes darting everywhere, he threaded a path through the nearby trees and bushes until he entered a small clearing. Here two horses stood, their reins trailing, and between them George Binns lay flat upon his back.

Walking up to the supine figure, Creed bent over and gazed down into a pair of glazing eyes. He realised then that Binns must have been more seriously hurt than he had supposed, for the man was almost certainly dead now. He began a search for signs of life nevertheless, but there were none present, and he straightened his back again quite sure that Binns had indeed expired. His end must have come just after Norton and he had entered the trees, and the former would have lost time in going through the same examination that Creed had just performed.

Yet the fact of the manager's death did nothing to explain Norton's subsequent behaviour. Indeed, in practical terms, Binns' demise had freed Norton of all responsibility for the man and provided him with the opportunity to speed up his escape and do everything he could to elude his hunter. It seemed most probable that he had turned on Creed with the intention of eliminating the pursuit then and there, but had found out, in the middle of attacking the railroad detective that he was too badly wounded to go anywhere. Why else should he have sought death? Because that was what he appeared to have done. And that had been strangely defeatist and not like Norton at all. Yes, Billy had perhaps cheated the gallows, but he had also cheated himself. That would always remain a mystery to Creed.

With some difficulty in his own weakened state, Creed loaded the dead men across the backs of their horses. Then, with the mounts on tow behind his own, he moved back in the direction of the railroad, hoping that the train bearing the county sheriff and his posse would soon come along, and he had not ridden too far eastwards when the loco-motive and three box cars did appear.

Creed waved the speeding engine down. Fortunately for him, Morgan Target, the county sheriff, was riding on the footplate and had the train stopped opposite where Creed sat. Target climbed down from the locomotive, and a fairly brief conversation took place into which the railroad detective compressed the tale of his long and hazardous day, adding that the line was blocked in Cutman's Pass and that the area adjacent was somewhat littered with human remains. 'That's it,' he said, when no important detail remained to be spoken. 'In the course of getting a job done, I've killed a lot of men, and I'm your prisoner if you see it so.'

'Creed,' Target said bluntly, 'I don't like you – and I never will. But I see no cause to take you into custody. You seem to have done a remarkable job for the railroad and everybody else. That makes what I have to tell you all the easier – even pleasing.'

'Pleasing?' Creed queried, his eyebrows shooting upwards in surprise.

'Word from your head office in Des Moines,' Target explained. 'It seems they want you back on the active list at just about any price – as head of detectives.'

'But that's Monty Black's job.'

'He's been taken very ill, Creed. Heart attack. He nominated you his successor. That's as I had it from Union Pacific, and you now have it. So?'

'Thanks. I don't know yet. It's rather a shock.'

'In your place, I wouldn't spend too much time thinking it over.'

'I don't aim to,' Creed said deliberately.

'My posse and I will have to clean up in Cutman's Pass,' Target observed. 'Are you coming back to Cheyenne with us?'

'No, sir,' Creed responded. 'I have to make certain that the Flyer is stopped at Flegg's Halt tonight. Mustn't leave the smallest risk of a crash.'

'Creed, there's one man's share. Other people have to do their jobs too.'

Creed nodded. 'Still my responsibility. I have to call on a young woman also, and tell her that after a week of marriage she's a widow.'

'Madge Stacey?'

Creed gave his chin another jerk.

'How will she take that?'

'I wish to heck,' Creed said heavily, 'I could be sure. Women are mighty unpredictable. You imagine it one way – and they go the other.'

'Well, that's your business,' Target remarked tersely. 'I'm through that part of my life, and glad of it. You can leave those bodies with us. It's a good ride back to Flegg's Halt from here.'

'I shan't take much rocking tonight,' Creed yawned, smiling briefly. 'Thanks.' He turned his horse westwards, then spurred off, lifting his right hand in salute.

'Do try to stay out of trouble,' the county sheriff called after him in pained tones.

Creed grimaced at the sunset world up front. To stay out of trouble had always been his first aim and desire. But that wasn't what they paid him for – and a chief of detectives could hardly expect a quiet life. If he took the damned job; and he knew very well he would.

This Large Print Book for the partially sighted, who cannot read normal print, is published under the auspices of

THE ULVERSCROFT FOUNDATION